WEEP,
SHUDDER,
DIE

The Trinity Forum

WEEP, SHUDDER, DIE

On Opera and Poetry

DANA GIOIA

PAUL DRY BOOKS

Philadelphia   2024

First Paul Dry Books Edition, 2024

Paul Dry Books, Inc.
Philadelphia, Pennsylvania
www.pauldrybooks.com

Cover image: David Hobson as Rodolfo and Cheryl Barker as Mimì
in Opera Australia's *La Bohème*. Photograph by Philip Le Masurier,
reproduced by courtesy of the photographer. 1990.

Printed in the United States of America

Library of Congress Control Number: 2024946228
ISBN: 978-1-58988-196-9

For Paula Deitz

Our bright-eyed Athena

CONTENTS

PREFACE

Weep, Shudder, Die is an idiosyncratic book about the extravagant and alluring art of opera. The book does not discuss the subject in the usual ways. It doesn't present the history of opera as a musical art. It has nothing to say about singers, directors, or conductors. The focus is not primarily on music. This book looks at composers as collaborative artists working in a form different from other types of music—a mix of song, poetry, story, and spectacle—that depends on complex and precarious live performance to exist.

This book explores opera from the perspective by which it was originally created—as the most intense form of poetic drama. Opera has changed in many ways over the past four centuries, but the great works have never lost the essential connection to poetry, song, and the primal power of the human voice. All poetry was originally sung or chanted. It was even danced—the bodies of the singers portrayed the rhythms of the sound. Poetry and song were one art—public, communal, and ecstatic. Its aim, as Plato warned, was irrational enchantment, the unleashing of emotions and visionary imagination.

The literary elements of opera are misunderstood. There is an assumption that in opera words hardly matter, that great operas can be built on execrable texts. But the libretto is not a shabby coat rack on which the magnificent vestments of music are hung. Operas begin with their words. Strong words inspire composers, weak words burden them. Ultimately singers embody the words to give the music a human form for the audience.

This is a poet's book about opera. To some people, that statement will suggest writing that is airy, impressionistic, and unreliable, but a poet also brings a practical sense of how words animate opera, lend life to imaginary characters, and give human shape to music. And a poet knows about love. There is no art I love more than opera. I have written this book for those who, sharing the devotion, have wept in the dark of an opera house.

Dana Gioia

Through singing, opera must make you weep, shudder, die.

—VINCENZO BELLINI

CHAPTER I

The Librettist as Idiot

*The poet of the opera house and the idiot
were at a certain time synonymous
among the learned of London.*

—LORENZO DA PONTE (1819)

No POETIC GENRE RANKS LOWER IN LITERARY ESTEEM
than the opera libretto. It occupies an inglorious position roughly equal to defunct genres such as the pas-
toral eclogue or verse sermon. Contemporary readers
have few opinions on the mock epic, but they are well-
stocked with specific objections to the libretto. In the
English-speaking world, the verbal component of opera
is considered sub-literary. A libretto is a hodgepodge of
implausible plotting, hyperbolic characterization, and
incompetent versification.

It will not occur to most detractors that they have
never read a complete libretto in its original language.
If they have read one at all, it was probably in a poor,
antiquated, and severely cut translation. A few scholars
may celebrate the sophistication of operatic theater, but
for the general reader the libretto remains synonymous
with bad poetry and stilted drama.

Consider, however, that opera began as a literary project—the attempt in 1598 by the Florentine Camerata, a group of artists and intellectuals, to recreate the performance practices of classical Greek drama. The poetic text was primary. The music was designed to serve the words; composers therefore crafted a style simpler than the prevailing polyphony. The first operatic music featured plain vocal lines designed to project and underscore the verse. Compared to later operatic vocalism, the earliest operas sound less like singing than intoned declamation. It says everything about the Camerata's artistic priorities that the text of the first opera, Ottavio Rinuccini's *Dafne*, survives while most of Jacopo Peri and Jacopo Corsi's music has been lost.

No one today comes to the opera to hear the libretto; nor has any musical drama maintained a place in the repertory solely on the basis of its text. The literary aspect of opera has not disappeared—composers and singers need words—but poetic quality has become a minor consideration. As opera developed from its elite literary origins into a popular theatrical form, the priorities of the libretto changed; the subject, scenario, and characters gradually became more important than the lyrics. Opera is still considered a type of drama, but it has become a primarily musical medium in which the composer exercises controlling interest. In the Renaissance there was a passionate debate on the nature of opera. Intellectuals posed the question: *Prima la musica o prima le parole?* Does music take precedence or do the words? Today that question seems purely rhetorical.

Yet the question of opera's relation to poetry deserves to be asked again, if only to suggest the implausibility of conventional opinion. Can an intelligent observer accept the notion that the masterpieces of opera consist of great music and deplorable texts? Were these theatrical classics created by composers who set doggerel for stock characters in preposterous situations? Did the quality of the libretto play no meaningful role in the artistic outcome?

To give reasonable answers to these questions requires a nuanced understanding of collaborative art—not only opera but other theatrical forms such as ballet, film, and Broadway musicals. Literature is traditionally an affair of individual authorship, a single imagination expressing itself in words. "A great writer creates a world of his own," declared Cyril Connolly, "and his readers are proud to live in it." The vision of individual creation may apply to fiction and most poetry, but it is not a reliable perspective to understand a collaborative medium.

The human imagination tends to understand interdisciplinary arts by placing them in a single frame of reference. For opera, that frame is not literary but musical. The philosopher Susanne K. Langer argued that every work of art "has its being in only one order of art; compositions of different orders are not simply conjoined, but all except one will cease to appear as what they are." When two or more arts collaborate, she argues, one art form does not merely dominate, but subsumes the others. "Music ordinarily swallows words and action creating (thereby) opera, oratorio, or song."

I resisted Langer's view when I first encountered it forty years ago, but I now recognize, from personal observation, that she was right. Most people need a single frame of reference when they encounter a work of art. In Langer's terms, opera is a theatrical form of music shaped by the composer. Her statement may be accurate, but a frame of reference only explains the perspective of the audience. It isn't an adequate account of how opera expresses its full meaning. Nor does it include the finer distinctions that separate opera from other forms of music. Nor, finally, does it illuminate how an opera comes into being as a collaborative enterprise.

The audience experiences operatic music differently from a piano concerto or string quartet. It is not merely a matter of the singing, the spectacle, or the acting. Even on a recording of an unfamiliar work, the listener recognizes opera because it sounds different from symphonic or choral works. It moves in ways that are not internally motivated by musical ideas but arrive from external elements. Those elements are literary, theatrical, and poetic. Those features may not dominate opera's identity, but they help shape both the music and the audience's experience of it. That is one reason why musicologists so often dislike opera: it doesn't behave like proper music should.

Opera's musical identity accounts for why the art has traveled internationally to be appreciated by audiences who do not know the language of the libretto.

But it does not explain the discomfort an audience would feel if singers put on the costumes for *Aida* and proceeded to sing *Carmen*. Opera conveys meaning through costumes, acting, and scenery as well as words. Music may dominate opera, but the form remains a theatrical experience, even for people who don't understand the words. People expect to understand, at least in general terms, the narrative and characters. A minor change in the dramatic cohesion confuses their perception of the dramatic action.

The disjunction between what the libretto intends and what the performance presents has been exploited by contemporary directors who deliberately violate the libretto's instructions to reshape the theatrical content of works. This revisionist aesthetic, *Regietheater* ("Director's Theater"), seeks to break the original unity between the musical and literary elements. By deconstructing the literary elements—they don't dare change the musical score—directors hope to uncover or create new meanings. In the process they force audiences to intellectualize the experience of opera by placing commentary (often heavy-handed and sometimes incoherent) between them and the musical drama. Wotan stands on stage dressed as a banker, and leather-clad Valkyries drive in on motorcycles. The trend's popular nickname, "Eurotrash opera," suggests that audiences find little value in mutilating the libretto for a directorial concept. Most people go to opera to experience musical drama, not to puzzle through deconstructive commentary. Opera lovers want ecstasy, not instruction.

The Muse sometimes reveals her will through irony. At the same time directors were discarding the libretto, technology reinforced the importance of the words. The invention of theatrical surtitles by Toronto's Canadian Opera Company in 1983 allowed audiences to follow the text, moment by moment, during a performance. Within a decade, surtitles became an international convention. A simultaneous translation was now available, often in multiple languages, for every line the performers sang. The technology did not change opera's musical frame of reference, but it heightened the form's poetic aspects. Technology had made twenty-first-century opera almost as literary as its Renaissance prototype.

CHAPTER II

Music by the Book

How can I work without a libretto?
—GIOACHINO ROSSINI

WHAT MAKES AN OPERATIC MASTERPIECE? EVERYONE agrees it is the music. No opera continues to be performed in posterity without a compelling score. If the music is the key, however, why did some of the greatest lyric composers—Schubert, Mendelssohn, Schumann, Brahms and Mahler, for instance—fail to compose a successful opera? Why did a musical behemoth such as Beethoven have so much trouble completing *Fidelio*, his only opera? "I assure you," he wrote to his third librettist, "that this opera will win me a martyr's crown." He succeeded only after ten years of labor and several revisions. Were the problems musical? Could there be any musical challenge that Beethoven and the others could not solve? History suggests a different explanation for their difficulties with the form.

The historical record reveals the importance of the libretto in securing an opera's place in posterity. Anyone who studies international performance statistics discovers two interesting facts about the core repertory—

one obvious, the other not. First, as every operagoer knows, the standard repertory is dominated by a small number of composers. In any given year, half of the top one hundred works produced internationally generally come from only seven composers—Giuseppe Verdi, Giacomo Puccini, Wolfgang Amadeus Mozart, Richard Wagner, Gaetano Donizetti, Richard Strauss, and Gioachino Rossini. In fact, fifteen of the top twenty-five most widely performed operas are usually by only three composers—Puccini, Mozart, and Verdi. Those statistics suggest that composers determine the success of an opera.

There is, however, a second fact about the international repertory that goes unnoticed: the same statistics demonstrate the importance of the librettist. The most popular operas come from an equally small group of poets. Composers create their best work when given their best texts. Mozart's most popular Italian operas—*Don Giovanni, Le Nozze di Figaro,* and *Così Fan Tutte*—all have libretti by Lorenzo Da Ponte. (Mozart wrote nine other less popular operas in Italian with texts by other authors.) All but one of Richard Strauss's most performed operas have words by Hugo von Hofmannsthal.

Vincenzo Bellini doesn't make the uppermost echelon of composers in terms of performances. Only two of his operas usually rank in the top hundred, but his short career illustrates the significance of the librettist. His two classic works, *Norma* and *La Sonnambula*, both have words by Felice Romani. Wagner, who disliked most Italian opera, idolized Bellini as a composer who perfectly combined words and music. Bellini refused to work with any poet other than Romani, whose elegant verse inspired him. It is difficult to translate Romani's poetry without losing the sorcery of his word music. The sound is the meaning, the mood, and the magic that attracted Bellini. Listen to the opening lines of the Druid priestess Norma's aria to the moon. (I provide a literal translation which I urge readers to ignore.)

Casta Diva, che inargenti,
queste sacre antiche piante,
a noi volgi il bel sembiante,
senza nube e senza vel.

[Chaste goddess, who ensilvers
These holy ancient trees
Turn your beautiful countenance to us,
Unclouded and unveiled.]

Bellini set these verses as a *cavatina*, a simple melodious air without repeats or showy vocal effects. The piece was so slow and otherworldly that his prima donna, the famed Giuditta Pasta, rejected it. She expected a more virtuosic entrance. Bellini agreed to compose a new aria if she still wanted one after practicing *"Casta Diva"* for a week. Pasta became the first of countless sopranos who fell under its spell. The *cavatina* survives as a signature aria of the bel canto period.

Bellini knew the importance of the right librettist. He made impresarios double Romani's normal fee to secure his involvement. The extra money was also nec-essary for the librettist to endure the temperamental composer. Bellini once sent the police to harass the poet when he was late with copy. (No wonder Romani even-tually broke off their partnership.) Bellini was not alone in recognizing the synergy Romani brought to musical drama. The poet was in constant demand and worked with every major Italian composer of the era, including Donizetti, Rossini, and Verdi.

Half of the international standard repertory (twenty-four of the fifty most frequently performed operas) are the work of only eight poets—Lorenzo Da Ponte, Felice Romani, Francesco Maria Piave, Salvadore Camma-rano, Arrigo Boito, Luigi Illica, Hugo von Hofmanns-thal, and Richard Wagner. These authors often worked in partnership with a particular composer. The stellar creative teams were Mozart/Da Ponte, Bellini/Romani, Verdi/Piave, Verdi/Boito, Puccini/Illica, and Strauss/ Hofmannsthal. Wagner is a special case. The master of Bayreuth wrote all of his own libretti.

Performance statistics and rankings bother some people. How can great art be so crudely judged by pop-ularity? International performance history, however, provides a measure of objectivity to subjective critical preferences. (I compiled my list by averaging interna-tional performance statistics across thirty years—an almost unnecessary methodology since the top fifty operas remained nearly unchanged over that period; only the internal rankings shifted slightly—as the same favorites moved up or down a few steps.) It is significant that a small cohort of operas has dominated the repertory for decades, even centuries, despite changes in taste and fashion. Certain operas foster such passion that they are presented year after year. The motive isn't institutional greed. All opera companies lose money, even when the house sells out. As Molière quipped, "Of all the noises known to man, opera is the most expensive." The popularity of the great repertory operas reflects the love and sustained fascination of impresarios, artists, and audiences.

The importance of certain librettists becomes clear in studying the historical data. There were, for example, approximately ten thousand Italian operas produced in what William Weaver called the "Golden Century." (Weaver's "century" spans the one hundred and ten years between the premieres of Rossini's *The Barber of Seville* in 1816 and Puccini's posthumous *Turandot* in 1926.) Discussing this period when Italy produced a steady stream of new works that captured an international audience, Weaver neglected to note one startling fact: the majority of the operas still regularly performed have libretti by only five poets—Romani, Piave, Boito, Illica, and Cammarano. Their verse had a special power to inspire composers to lyric excellence. But why limit their creative influence to their verse? These poets also shaped characters, devised plots, and crafted dramatic situations that moved and enchanted audiences. Great librettists are as rare as great composers.

One might hypothesize that the librettists succeeded because they had the luck to work with the right composers. Indeed, it was serendipitous for a poet to collaborate with a genius such as Verdi, though it may not have felt that way during the composer's many temper tantrums. The success of the master librettists, however, was not limited to their collaboration with the five composers who dominate the Italian repertory—Donizetti, Bellini, Verdi, Rossini, and Puccini. These poets also wrote libretti for other composers or themselves. Their participation had a measurable effect on the success of minor composers. The single operas that survive in the international repertory by Amilcare Ponchielli and Umberto Giordano each had a libretto by one of these five poets.

Boito not only wrote the text for his own repertory opera, *Mefistofele*. He also crafted the libretti for Verdi's *Otello, Falstaff,* and the radically revised *Simon Boccanegra*, as well as Ponchielli's *La Gioconda*. One poet, therefore, wrote the texts for five of the most popular operas by three different composers. Luigi Illica wrote the libretti for Puccini's *Tosca, La Bohème,* and *Madama Butterfly,* aided by Giuseppe Giacosa whose job it was to improve Illica's rough verse. These perennially popular works make Puccini the only composer who usually holds three spots on the list of top ten most widely performed operas. Illica also wrote the text for Giordano's greatest success, *Andrea Chénier,* as well as two minor operas that survive on the margins of the repertory, Pietro Mascagni's *Iris* and Alfredo Catalani's *La Wally*.

Ruggero Leoncavallo does not make the inner circle of top composers or librettists. He could never repeat the huge success of his first work, *Pagliacci*, but he demonstrated a keen literary gift in both his own operas and his work with other musicians. He was an excellent poet who had studied in Bologna with Giosuè Carducci, the first Italian to win the Nobel Prize in literature. Leoncavallo not only wrote the libretto for his own *Pagliacci* (1892), but he also collaborated with Puccini on the text for *Manon Lescaut* (1893). He, therefore, wrote the words for two of the most popular operas. In *Pagliacci* Leoncavallo also crafted—in addition to the original story, lyrics, and music—what is arguably the most famous moment in all opera—"*Vesti la giubba*." In this aria the weeping clown Canio applies his comic make-up after discovering his wife's infidelity. (Enrico Caruso's 1902 version became the first record ever to sell a million copies.) Leoncavallo later wrote the music and words for his own adaptation of Henri Murger's *La Bohème* (1897). His charming lyrical version was obliterated by Puccini's nearly simultaneous masterpiece.

Nearly everyone, highbrow or lowbrow, still believes in the Romantic notion of the artist as an individual creative force. Notions of collaborative art remain difficult to comprehend. Collaboration implies creative compromise or dilution of individual vision. Great art surely requires the heroic assertion of individuality, whatever the cost. This Romantic notion makes little sense to people who work in musical theater or opera. Lyric theater does not merely survive partnership; the art emerges from the energy different personalities bring together. Opera requires more than the simple binary model of musical journalism, which generally considers only the composer (the lone gunman of the creative act) and the singers who bring the work to life. Operas begin with words. There is no opera without a libretto.

The ability of the right lyricist to focus a theatrical composer would not surprise a Broadway producer. Most theatrical scores are done by creative teams, and great teams write multiple hits—George and Ira Gershwin, Richard Rodgers and Oscar Hammerstein, Alan Jay Lerner and Frederick Loewe, and, more recently, Alan Menken and Howard Ashman (which ended with Ashman's early death from AIDS). Great lyricists galvanize a composer. A single team, W. S. Gilbert and Arthur Sullivan, holds a near monopoly on the British operetta repertory—the only operatic partnership in which the librettist gets top billing.

Successful collaboration generates a result not only greater but different from the sum of the parts. Neither Gilbert nor Sullivan ever created works separately comparable to what they achieved together, despite their temperamental and unstable partnership. They also profited from an extended artistic partnership with the D'Oyly Carte Opera Company. The alliance let them write for a fixed ensemble of singers for whom they could tailor both the lyrics and music. Such working conditions might seem restrictive to true believers of the Romantic myth. But opera only fully exists in performance. There is no way to realize the composer's intentions without the singers. Rossini, Donizetti, and Verdi crafted many of their greatest roles to suit specific voices.

Even one-time collaborations can create singular results. Jule Styne never wrote a better musical than *Gypsy*, his one partnership with Stephen Sondheim as lyricist. The energy that came when Rodgers teamed up with Hammerstein (after the death of his first lyricist, Lorenz Hart) is not so different from what Mozart found in Da Ponte. The right partnership enhances creativity. Literary quality focuses compositional genius, even for a Mozart. *Prima la musica*, to be sure, but *anche le parole*. The best vocal music is called into existence by the right words.

CHAPTER III

The Librettist as Guide

The job of the librettist is to furnish the
composer with a plot, characters, and words:
of these the least important, so far as the
audience is concerned, is words.

—W. H. AUDEN

IF THE POET IS THE SUBORDINATE PARTNER IN OPERA, THE
librettist has nonetheless often been the decisive pro-
vocateur of artistic change. Christoph Willibald Gluck
earned his pivotal role in the history of opera by advo-
cating radical reform of the art. He championed a return
to the simplicity, continuity, and humanity of classical
drama after the virtuosic display and theatrical excesses
of Baroque opera. The verse of the libretto, Gluck
insisted, needed to be heard clearly rather than lost in
vocal fireworks. He condemned any theatrical effect not
contributing to the perfect union of the music and text.

Those famous notions, published in the preface to
Gluck's *Alceste* (1767), however, did not originate with
the composer. They came from his librettist Ranieri de'
Calzabigi, who convinced the composer to change his
aesthetic. Calzabigi even served as ghostwriter for the

composer's historic manifesto. Just as the poet's name often gets left off the opera program, so, too does it get left out of music history.

Much of the librettist's influence goes unrecorded. Most operas begin with the composer and poet talking about the subject, characters, and approach. The librettist learns what elements excite the composer's imagination, and the composer considers new artistic possibilities. In his three collaborations with Mozart, the Venetian poet Lorenzo Da Ponte brought the composer a comic sophistication and thematic complexity beyond his earlier theatrical works. Little documentation survives for this sudden and historic transformation, but there was likely some coaching by Da Ponte to help the composer of the cartoonish *Abduction from the Seraglio* become the magus of *Don Giovanni*.

Da Ponte had the most interesting life of any librettist. He was a Jewish-born Catholic priest of relaxed morals and high literary ambition. A professor of literature, he wrote poetry in both Latin and Italian. One of his closest friends was Giacomo Casanova, and Padre Da Ponte was not discreet in the escapades they shared. He was eventually banished from Venice for living in a brothel and "abducting a respectable woman." With the help of Antonio Salieri, Da Ponte came to Vienna to serve as the Latin secretary and theater poet for the Holy Roman Emperor, Joseph II. In the Hapsburg capital, Da Ponte met Mozart, a composer of consummate genius and limited literary taste. Together they crafted—in quick succession—Mozart's three finest

Italian operas, indeed three of the greatest operas ever written—*Le Nozze di Figaro* (1786), *Don Giovanni* (1787) and *Così Fan Tutte* (1790). At the death of Joseph II, Da Ponte was dismissed. He struggled for employment in Dresden, Prague, Paris, and London. He wrote the last of his twenty-eight libretti in London. In 1805 he fled his debtors by emigrating to the United States with his mistress and their children. After working as a green-grocer in Pennsylvania, he came to New York where he opened a bookstore and became the first professor of Italian at Columbia College. (He received no salary but collected fees as a tutor.) Da Ponte bears the unique distinction of being both the first Catholic priest and first Jew to join the Columbia faculty. In 1825 he produced the American premiere of *Don Giovanni*. At seventy-nine he became an American citizen. In 1833, when he was eighty-four years old, he launched an opera company and helped build the first opera house in America. Two seasons later it went bankrupt. When Da Ponte died in 1838, escaping his debtors one last time, he was given an elaborate funeral at St. Patrick's Cathedral. On the basis of his final nationality, one is tempted to declare him America's greatest librettist.

Vienna saw a similar transformation in the early twentieth century when Hugo von Hofmannsthal began his long collaboration with Richard Strauss. Hofmannsthal's theatrical vision led Strauss to artistic growth the composer would not have achieved independently. (Strauss was a genius in music but thick-headed in nearly everything else, especially politics.) Hofmannsthal's catalytic influence is documented in letters; he enticed, encouraged, and chided the composer into creative refinement and exploration.

In opera the words come first, so they have the potential to guide the music into new artistic territory. Pietro Metastasio (1698–1782), the most celebrated librettist ever, took this notion to the extreme. The poet not only picked the operatic subject and crafted the text; he also suggested what sort of music the composer should write, including the orchestral passages. Composers in that practical, pre-Romantic age listened to suggestions from Europe's top lyricist. Metastasio's name on a new opera gave it dramatic credibility.

Metastasio's success was immediate and enduring. His early verse was so beguiling that the noisy Neapolitan audience stayed quiet to hear each word. The grace and musicality of his arias still astonishes. Here is an aria from *Siroe, Re di Persia*, a libretto set by George Frideric Handel, Antonio Vivaldi, Johann Adolf Hasse, and others:

L'onda che mormora
tra sponda e sponda,
l'aura che tremola
tra fronda e fronda,
è meno instabile
del vostro cor.

Pur l'alme semplici
de' folli amanti

sol per voi spargono
sospiri e pianti,
e da voi sperano
fede in amor.

[The waves that murmur
from shore to shore,
the air that trembles
from bough to bough,
is less volatile.
than your heart.

Yet the simple soul,
mad with love
for you alone, scatters
sighs and cries,
and hopes for your
faith in love.]

Metastasio's libretti presented noble stories from classical history and mythology. He created a tight dramatic structure that shaped both music and action. The plots progressed in carefully planned series of elegant arias, each of which dramatized the shifting psychological state of the characters. In the finale, the dangerous conflicts of the plot were resolved by the intervention of a beneficent deity or monarch. These tragic situations that turned out to have happy endings were called *opera seria* ("serious opera"). Metastasio's dignified and stately operas, adorned with exquisite poetry, were perfectly suited for Enlightenment Europe. Their popular appeal did not survive Romanticism.

Metastasio worked with almost every significant opera composer of his time and continued to have his libretti set posthumously. Vivaldi, Handel, Gluck, Haydn, Mozart, and Donizetti all wrote operas to his texts, as did many now-neglected *maestri* such as Hasse, Galuppi, Jommelli, Porpora, Salieri, and Cherubini—a Who's Who of late Baroque and early Classical composers. Metastasio's twenty-seven heroic *opera serie* were set to music 800 times by 300 composers. He lived to eighty-four and spent his last fifty years in Vienna as the court poet of the Holy Roman Empire. Never before or since would a poet exercise such an influence on opera. Metastasio may be the only librettist to have a monument erected in his honor. Elegantly dressed, with pen in hand, he still stands in front of the *Chiesa Nuova* (*Santa Maria in Vallicella*) in Rome.

Two centuries later, Bertolt Brecht transformed Kurt Weill's musical career with his caustic, comic libretto for *Die Dreigroschenoper* (*The Threepenny Opera*)— their 1928 adaptation of John Gay's *The Beggar's Opera* (1728). They mixed classical, cabaret, and avant-garde elements to create a startling yet appealing theatrical work. Weill spent the rest of his life in musical theater. He and Brecht later produced *Rise and Fall of the City of Mahagonny* (1930) and the "sung ballet" *The Seven Deadly Sins* (1933). Neither work proved as popular as their international blockbuster *The Threepenny Opera*, but both have kept a foothold in the repertory. Each artist went on to do fine work independently, but neither ever found a partner to create a comparable masterpiece. Brecht's next opera, *The Condemnation of Lucullus* (1951) with music by Paul Dessau, was a joyless dud, even by the grim standards of Communist East Germany. Weill later collaborated with a panoply of literary talents, including Franz Werfel, Maxwell Anderson, Langston Hughes, Ira Gershwin, and Ogden Nash. He composed timeless songs but never created another enduring theatrical work.

CHAPTER IV

Opera as Export

*Song gives voice to what can't normally
be heard: the language of the soul,
or of the unconscious mind.*

—PETER CONRAD

THE RELATIONSHIP BETWEEN WORDS AND MUSIC HAS never been stable in opera. One significant change occurred in the mid-seventeenth century when opera became an international art form—one of the many luxury goods Italy exported. The works were now presented to audiences who mostly did not speak Italian. (The convention that opera be presented in Italian was so strong that for nearly two centuries even Germanic composers such as Handel, Mozart, and Haydn wrote operas in Italian.) This situation—slowly but decisively—influenced the nature of the texts. In his *Vie de Rossini* (1824), Stendhal speculated that one reason for the international success of Italian opera was that the foreign audience needed to understand only a few words or phrases from an aria to apprehend its meaning. Music and staging did the rest. Opera still depended on drama, but poetry was no longer a necessary component for foreign audiences.

The rise of Italian Romantic opera further diminished the status verse had enjoyed in the Classical period. Watching Rossini's operas, Stendhal noted the shift in the expressive relation between words and music. Rossini's melodies no longer focused on projecting the poetic text. Instead, his music concerned itself with creating a dramatic moment in which the lyrics were only one element. The narrative situation was often conveyed as a sort of symphonic pantomime triggered by a few key words—*amore, padre, terrore, gioia, morte*. Opera had changed from poetic drama to introductory Italian.

Verdi perfected the expressive method of fragmenting verse into isolated phrases repeated for dramatic effect. He cut his libretti to find these evocative verbal units with little regard to textual integrity. He knew his music would provide the necessary unity. "In other words," writes musicologist Rodolfo Celletti, "significant melody gives significance even to words which in and of themselves do not have it." In *La Traviata*, each time its tragic heroine Violetta sings the words "*È strano*" ("It's strange"), Verdi's music cunningly recapitulates her emotional history. Verdi eventually made this notion of key words and phrases central to his dramatic planning. He designed whole acts around *sceniche parole* (pictorial words). Those musical phrases served a similar thematic function in his operas to the *leitmotifs* in Wagner's. The technique proved so theatrically effective that it changed the librettist's role. Endowed by music with special meaning, the phrase could now become more important than the line or stanza.

Outside Italy, an odd but still familiar situation continued; audiences heard poetic drama sung in languages they didn't understand. This obstacle did not diminish opera's appeal. It remained Europe's most popular and prestigious form of music or theater. The language barrier, however, gave opera the aura of foreign authority. Germans were obliged to use Italian libretti for everything except light comedy—a situation which suggested that the German language wasn't up to the task of the high style. For many northern musicians and writers, their love of opera was mixed with envy and resentment. They hungered to create stirring and mighty works in their own tongue.

CHAPTER V

A Brief Note on Romanticism

Music is a higher revelation
than all wisdom and philosophy.

—LUDWIG VAN BEETHOVEN

ROMANTICISM MARKED A TURNING POINT IN THE HISTORY
of opera. The form became both fully international and
deeply nationalistic. For the first time, serious operas
were written in each country's vernacular, and the art
form became a vehicle for national identity. New styles
and genres of opera also emerged from that cultural
and political shift.

The complex change of style, sensibility, and values
known as Romanticism began in Germany and England
in the late eighteenth century, and then it slowly spread
across Europe and the Americas. No one has ever ade-
quately defined Romanticism, the term is too protean
and capacious. Even after two hundred years of critical debate, the movement looks different from different
vantage points. To take only one example: Johann von
Goethe's *Faust* is generally considered the central masterpiece of European Romanticism, but Germans don't
classify the work as Romantic. Among the few points

of critical agreement is that Romanticism took a different form in each country and was in every case decisively shaped by poetry and verse drama. In Germany, where music had long enjoyed a special status in intellectual culture, the sudden emergence of great poetry in the age of Goethe, Schiller, Hölderlin, and Heine had an explosive cultural effect.

Romanticism transformed German opera by inspiring German composers and poets to write serious opera in their own languages. (Until then, only comic operas with spoken dialogue, *Singspiel*, had been written in German.) This shift charged the form with nationalistic energy. As the various German states slowly moved toward unification, the emerging nation sought its collective identity in its myths, legends, and folktales. New libretti used folkloric material with supernatural and even religious elements alien to the Italian sensibility. This visionary and nationalistic tradition went from Carl Maria Weber's *Der Freischütz* (1821) to Wagner's *Der Ring des Nibelungen* (1869–1876). It continued in works such as Engelbert Humperdinck's *Königskinder* (1910) to Carl Orff's *Der Mond* (1939) until the Third Reich and its fall made German nationalist mythmaking artistically impossible.

The development of German Romantic opera also faced a paradoxical impediment from poetry itself. The radiant rise of German poetry in the late eighteenth and early nineteenth century excited the imagination of composers. A new musical and poetic art form, the *lied* or art song, suddenly emerged as a major artistic

medium. For nearly a century the best German composers—Schubert, Schumann, Mendelssohn, Brahms,
Wolf, and Mahler—set the best of German poetry to
music. Meanwhile manufacturing innovation made
pianos affordable for middle-class homes, which gave
songs for voice and piano a huge constituency of both
amateur and professional musicians While Italian
operas played to non-Italian audiences in theaters from
St. Petersburg and London to Cairo and Buenos Aires,
lieder filled the parlors of the German-speaking world.
This compact but expressive form slowly spread across
the nations of Europe—with one notable exception. The
art song never became a major genre in Italy.

Once music became the ascendant element in Romantic opera, the role of the poet changed again. The
librettist became less concerned with lyrics than with
grand themes, theatrical effect, and even national identity. In theory, there is nothing wrong with such a broad
view of the librettist's goals. Neither Shakespeare nor
Schiller conceived of verse drama as a purely poetic
performance. Their plays were driven by plot, characters, dramatic situations, and theme, all articulated
through verse. In the new world of Romantic opera
those other elements remained, but they were now increasingly articulated by the music. As Patrick J. Smith
comments in *The Tenth Muse* (1970), his astute historical study of the libretto, this shift:

> necessitated a different evaluation of the qualities of the
> librettist, for he no longer was primarily a poet to be

judged by the musicality of his lines and aptness of his rhythms, rhymes, and similes. The librettist had become more: he had become a dramatist as well. . . . To consider the librettist merely a poet is to denigrate his function in the creation of an opera, for in the vast majority of cases the librettist supplied the original, motive force for the composition of the opera and created the dramatic node around which the final work was constructed.

In other words, the librettist had returned to the poet's original role in Florentine opera; the lyric dramatist created the story, characters, words, and theatrical style of the work. The composer animated those elements through music. Although still inferior to composers, the poets had reclaimed some of their traditional powers.

CHAPTER VI

The Imaginary Operagoer

There is nothing like youth.
The middle-aged are mortgaged to Life.

—OSCAR WILDE

THERE WAS SOMETHING SHAMEFUL ABOUT LOVING OPERA. Especially for a boy. Opera was pretentious, boring, effete, and effeminate. By the time I was ten I understood the unsavory reputation of the art. Opera represented everything that my childhood in postwar America asked me not to be.

I had never been to the opera. I had never even seen an opera house, except in old movies. I knew from the Marx Brothers' *A Night at the Opera* that rich people went there, but they didn't much enjoy it. Only Groucho had any fun. The patrons were old and overweight— bejeweled matrons and potbellied bankers stuffed into tuxedos. There was also something sinister about opera's orgy of opulence. In Lon Chaney's *The Phantom of the Opera*, the opera house was built over the city sewers. A mad composer emerged from this mephitic underworld to kidnap and kill. He wore elegant clothes, including an opera cape, but without his stylish mask, he was a monster. Opera was somehow both tedious and malevolent.

I wasn't sure why opera provoked such distaste. It went beyond dislike, class prejudice, or xenophobia. It roused a sort of moral suspicion. There was something weak or unhealthy about an operagoer. What sort of person craves oversized emotions sung in foreign languages? What grown man could be so soft and sensitive? Such a creepy passion wasn't normal. The Puritans, who colonized America, banned theater as sinful. If plays were emblems of depravity, what would they have thought of opera with its amplification of violent affection and sexual desire? Opera was sheer depravity, witchcraft so strong it crossed language barriers—a foul and foreign vice only Catholics could have devised.

I was raised among Italians and Mexicans, all deeply Catholic, even the atheists. Yet they half agreed with the Puritans. Opera crossed some boundary. It might not be depraved, but it was virulent in its pretention and sentimentality. In 1960, America was still a Puritan country. Everything in a boy's education focused on making him manly. The official culture of my youth sponsored Cub Scouting, team sports, and church service as altar boys. Street culture provided schoolyard fights, bullying, and neighborhood gangs. There was no escaping manhood, responsible or otherwise, without persecution and disgrace.

I realized the dangers of opera too late to be saved. By ten I had already been corrupted by my parents.

Neither of them had ever been to the opera. The notion would have struck them as absurd. But they loved singing, and that included the operatic arias they heard on variety shows. Back then opera stars were frequent guests on radio and television. There were about two dozen operatic standards that everyone knew. Even Bugs Bunny sang them.

For my father, opera was also a source of tribal pride. It was one of many reasons why Italian civilization was the greatest in the world. In the same way, he reveled in the accomplishments of Italian American athletes—Joe DiMaggio, Rocky Marciano, Eddie Arcaro. He was less informed on opera, yet he had two heroes—Enrico Caruso and Mario Lanza. My father invoked Caruso as the greatest singer who ever lived. It was an opinion that brooked no dissent in our household. My father didn't know that Lanza wasn't really an opera singer, but Lanza had starred in *The Great Caruso*. That was good enough for my dad.

At unpredictable intervals my handsome father put on an old Caruso record. He would sit me beside him next to the turntable, and we would listen to one or two cuts—crackly ancient performances of *"Vesti la giubba"* or *"Celeste Aida."* Then he lifted the needle. A little opera went a long way—about the same amount of music he would have heard on *The Ed Sullivan Show*. He never said much, but this record was one of the few things he ever shared with me in a formal way. He had given up trying to interest me in baseball or boxing.

I assumed all Italians liked opera. My grandfather

lived in the apartment next door. He was a tough immigrant who had survived many hardships, including hassles with the local police and the mob, neither of whom he would pay off. I admired him enormously. One day when he came over, I put on an opera recording. I thought he would be proud of me for liking Italian culture. He walked in, listened for a moment, and then bleated like an animal in time with the music. As I turned off the record, he howled with laughter at his ridiculous grandson. I never repeated the mistake with any other relation.

My father had no musical training, but he had a good ear. He had been a championship dancer before he joined the Navy in World War II. He had won the "Mr. Jitterbug" contest in Los Angeles. With it came a chance to dance in the movies. He quit Hollywood after two days. It took too much effort to be a star. After the war, he courted my mother by taking her to jazz clubs. As newlyweds, they went to dance halls and after-hours clubs. They bet on the horses at Hollywood Park. All the fun ended, my mother often remarked, when I arrived.

The house was still full of music. My parents had a stack of 78s. Some nights they put on a record to dance in our little kitchen. Making coffee, my dad would sing "Java Jive." Drying the dishes, he crooned, "I don't get around much anymore." "No," my mom would answer, "we don't."

I was a nocturnal child. My mother worked nights. She got home at 2 a.m. and slept till noon. I went to bed late and read until midnight. I was an only child for seven years, and my parents treated me as a young adult, especially after my brother Ted was born. No one ever asked me to turn off the light. It was an illicit freedom no other child I knew enjoyed. When I remember the happiness of my childhood, much consists of the books I read at night. I can still recall the particular pleasures of *The Time Machine*, *Gulliver's Travels*, *Martian Chronicles*, or *At the Earth's Core*.

I was usually late to school. The nuns complained, but my parents didn't respond. I was an outstanding student, so the Sisters of Providence made allowances. They assumed I came from a troubled home. My mother seemed suspicious. She never took part in parish activities. They never guessed how odd she really was. When we did housework together, she recited poems.

My parents worked multiple jobs, but they were usually broke. Indigence didn't bother them; it was the natural state of things. They happily spent everything they made. We even ate in restaurants once a week. This extravagance was a topic of conversation among our relations. My folks weren't like other parents. In a world of ants, I was raised by two grasshoppers. I felt loved and secure. I didn't yet know that ants ruled the planet.

At school I soon realized that I was different from the other boys. I had no interest in sports. I avoided group activities. I was the only boy in my class who chose not to be an altar boy. It wasn't a religious statement. I was mildly pious. I just didn't want to get up early to serve at Mass. My parents barely made the noon service, what the Irish called "the drunkard's

Mass." Most Sundays I went to church alone. I didn't mind. I never minded doing things alone.

In my working-class Los Angeles neighborhood, boy culture was violent and hierarchical. Most of the misbehavior was mindless anarchy. The older boys smashed or defaced things—it didn't matter what. But their cruelty repelled me. They persecuted weaker and younger kids. They pelted stray cats with stones. We were supposed to fall in line. It was the Baby Boom. The back streets and alleys belonged to the young and aggressive. There were too many of us for the adults to supervise or control.

I was an awkward, dreamy boy, but I was big for my age and stubborn. I never picked a fight, but when pushed around, I fought back ferociously, even against older kids. I didn't need to win. I just had to be too much trouble to bully. I was left alone. That was my first inkling that what I wanted wasn't power but freedom. Two smart but nerdy Mexican kids gathered under my putative protection. They became my friends, but they weren't like me. There didn't seem to be anyone like me.

I was moved and motivated by different things from my classmates. Other kids either seemed not to notice or mocked the things that moved me deeply. When I heard certain music or poems, they would leave me breathless. When I looked at reproductions of art—I had never been to a museum and seen any originals—they sent me into a reverie. Art cast a spell over me. It gave me more than simple pleasure. I felt the sense of my own existence enlarge in unaccountable ways. I wanted to stay in the enchantment. I hungered for more.

I preferred these sensory and sensual phantasms to the everyday reality of school life, and I knew that fact was so shameful it needed to be hidden. Back then I couldn't put my disability into words, but I felt it keenly. My habits were not just escapist pastimes. They were abnormal passions. I was a mutant, a monster of sensibility, a changeling with a freakish vulnerability to beauty. Years later I found a name for my debilitation— I was an aesthete.

Of course, other people liked music, but I didn't like what they did. I loathed the popular songs I heard on TV. Since both my parents worked, I often spent evenings next door with my grandparents or great aunt. Neither of the older women spoke English. Indeed, neither had ever learned to read or write. They watched variety shows. I cringed as they enjoyed Dean Martin, Sammy Davis Jr., Patti Page, or Rosemary Clooney. It wasn't just the older singers; I couldn't bear Elvis Presley, Ricky Nelson, or other "teen idols." I was a little snob, but I wasn't entirely wrong. Popular song was in a bad patch between the end of Tin Pan Alley and the birth of classic rock. The hit songs performed on TV were contrived, syrupy, and overblown. (Someone is already writing me an angry letter. I've learned you can't argue about rock 'n roll. Even the worst song is part of someone's emotional history.) It took puberty, Bob Dylan, and the Beatles to bring me to pop music— just in time for rock's golden era.

What I loved no one else cared for—classical music. I heard it first only in snatches in movies and cartoons. It had such a strong effect on me that I searched out more. Our apartment and garage unit were packed with books and records that had belonged to my Mexican uncle. He served in the Merchant Marine and shared my room when he was ashore. After he was killed in a plane crash, my parents sold most of his records. My mother kept two Chopin albums which she remembered him listening to—Dinu Lipatti's *Preludes* and Arthur Rubinstein's *Waltzes*.

I listened to Chopin in the empty apartment when my parents were at work. The exquisite pleasure the music gave me was mixed with an acute but abstract longing. My elation resembled the first stirrings of sexual desire, but it was less specific and had no easy outlet. I felt a desperate but enigmatic desire. I couldn't explain what I burned for, except that I wanted to be elsewhere. I wasn't sure what that meant. I had never been anywhere but Hawthorne, California.

There were also a few opera recordings in the garage, including a dusty box set of *Der Fliegende Holländer*. I listened only to the first side of the first record— the overture and opening chorus. There was no libretto. I had no idea what the male choir was singing, but these human voices from the doomed ship reached me differently from the orchestral music. I liked music with characters and a story, even if I didn't know the plot. Records were expensive. I took odd jobs and purchased albums from a tiny record shop a few blocks away. I looked through every classical record in their stock before making each purchase. It was a sort of education.

I found my uncle's *Victor Book of the Opera*. It had as many engrossing stories as Edith Hamilton's *Mythology*, which sat on the shelf next to it. *The Victor Book* described 110 "famous" operas, which flourished in some world I could hardly imagine but recognized from the movies. It was called New York. It didn't resemble the cold and hungry town my immigrant grandparents had fled. This New York was a city of bright lights and brilliant people who went to the opera and theater. I didn't expect ever to go there. Manhattan seemed as fabulous as Jonathan Swift's Lilliput or Laputa.

The book had been published before I was born. Much of the repertory it presented had already vanished, but I treated the antiquated table of contents as canonical. (After a lifetime of operagoing, I have never encountered a production of many of these former warhorses.) The names of these mysterious works, many in foreign languages, captivated me—*Fra Diavolo*, *L'Africaine*, *Twilight of the Gods*, *The King's Henchman*, *Le Prophète*, *The Golden Cockerel*. I read the plots and studied the photographs of costumed singers and sets. I reread the book so often I became an imaginary operagoer.

Like all young intellectuals, I formed strong opinions based on scant experience. Wagner was the greatest composer. His operas had dragons, heroes, magic swords, and giants as well as cursed captains and wandering knights. Their plot summaries were longer and more exciting than the others. How much better to have an opera present heroic myth than a love story. Any opera that featured the devil attracted my interest—*Faust*, *Mefistofele*, and the sensationally titled *La Damnation de Faust*. I had no idea what the music of *Faust* or *Der Ring des Nibelungen* sounded like, but I loved the idea of it. "Heard melodies are sweet but those unheard are sweeter." I was doomed.

I convinced my parents to join the RCA Victor record club. You got three free albums when you enrolled. I knew my father would support anything Italian. I chose highlights from *La Traviata* with Anna Moffo and *Aida* with Leontyne Price. My dad got *South Pacific*, which I loved nearly as much. After two months, my mother canceled the overpriced subscription, but by then I also had a small box set of great opera stars. I had discovered Verdi and fallen for Leontyne Price, my first *diva*. I listened to the records, alone in the apartment, after school. It didn't bother me that the voices sang in foreign languages. These were anthems from another world. I was now in the grip of a vice I have never been able to shake. While the other boys watched Sandy Koufax pitch for the Dodgers, I listened to Jussi Björling and Zinka Milanov sing Verdi.

Opera gave me the same bewildering pleasure that poetry did. Its beauty took me out of myself into the animating presence of something I craved but couldn't understand. Comprehension had nothing to do with it. What mattered was being in its presence. Real life seemed small and tongue-tied in comparison.

Years later, in college, I read Edgar Allan Poe's fervid discussion of poetic beauty in "The Poetic Principle." In the clinical atmosphere of Stanford's Senior Honors Seminar, Poe's rapturous tone and manner were embarrassing. Our professor advised us to skip over the passage and focus on the essay's central idea that no long poem can sustain the elevated excitement necessary for the art. And so I didn't pay attention. When I returned to the essay decades later, I saw that it described my own experience in opera and poetry better than anything I had ever found in contemporary criticism—not just my experience as a child but also as an adult.

I have an analytical frame of mind. I have always found the intellectual methods of arts criticism congenial, but academic criticism failed to acknowledge—perhaps even ignored—why poetry and music mattered to me. I wasn't seeking knowledge or wisdom; I wasn't even seeking pleasure. I wanted to surrender to an ecstasy beyond my control. Opera left me no wiser or happier. It just took me out of my ordinary self. Shamefully, that transient intoxication was enough. Poe knew the same helpless feeling:

It is the desire of the moth for the star. It is no mere appreciation of the Beauty before us—but a wild effort to reach the Beauty above. Inspired by an ecstatic prescience of the glories beyond the grave, we struggle, by multiform combinations among the things and thoughts of Time, to attain a portion of that Loveliness whose very elements, perhaps, appertain to eternity alone. And thus

when by Poetry,—or when by Music, the most entranc-
ing of the Poetic moods—we find ourselves melted into
tears—we weep then—not . . . through excess of pleasure,
but through a certain, petulant, impatient sorrow at our
inability to grasp *now*, wholly, here on earth, at once and
for ever, those divine and rapturous joys. . . .

Poe's diction makes me wince—*ecstatic prescience,
glories beyond the grave, divine and rapturous joy*. This
isn't just purple prose; it's imperial purple prose, too
lofty to worry about plebeian sense or linguistic deco-
rum. It must conquer the world or die in doomed battle.
Yet its emotional intensity gives it a visceral credibility. Poe has dropped any pretense to critical objectivity.
He struggles to describe something invisible, intan-
gible, unknowable. His prose becomes a prose poem
governed more by music than logic. Let all the adults
leave the room. I'm ten years old again and want to listen. I could defend this hyperbolic passage on historical grounds—these sentences helped inspire Charles
Baudelaire to create Symbolism, the catalyst of modern poetry. I prefer to defend it for inexcusably personal
reasons—Poe's rhapsodic outburst explains my petulant, impatient, sorrowful boyhood to my adult self. No
sensible description would have sufficed.

My conniving continued and worsened. When I
was eleven, my school was given four free tickets for
a Los Angeles Philharmonic youth concert featuring
selections from the *Ring*. I had already gone the year
before—the first time I ever heard a symphony orches-

tra—to hear Mussorgsky's *Pictures at an Exhibition*. There were 800 students at St. Joseph's, but I asked the sister who taught me piano if I could go again. She was appalled. She told me I was impossibly greedy and advised me to confess the sin. I knew she was right. My desire was selfish and disgraceful. I left her office embarrassed. On Saturday morning two hours before the concert, she called me. One of the chosen kids had decided not to go. While the other kids and parents sat bored beside me, I had the most thrilling musical experience of my young life. Being the only Wagnerite at St. Joseph's Parish School had its moral danger, but also its occasional bliss.

In the car home, I wanted to talk about the concert, but I knew it would be a mistake. Everyone else had already forgotten it. It was best to hide my enthusiasm. I had already been exposed as greedy. Why add weak and weird to the list? Many children lead secret lives. Mine was simply more elaborate than most. In public, I was an excellent student with an unpronounceable last name, a bit of a loner, terrible at sports. It was not a glamorous identity, but it was a manageable one. In private, I was a voluptuary who lived in his imagination fired by music, books, and art. I was never bored by solitude. I was preoccupied with things no one else liked.

Keeping my mouth shut in the back seat of the car was an important moment. I knew the practical people were right. To treat art as anything but a brief diversion was dangerous. It made everyday living more difficult. Beauty had an effect on me I didn't understand, but I recognized it made me cultivate a vulnerability that everyone else suppressed. There was no one to ask for advice. I could only wait and watch. Neither I nor the world was likely to change. I would find a way of leading two lives. Eventually there would be someone to talk to. Someday I would go to the opera.

CHAPTER VII

The Composer as Judge

*No good opera plot can be sensible, for people do
not sing when they are feeling sensible.*

—W. H. AUDEN

HOW DOES ONE JUDGE THE QUALITY OF AN OPERA
libretto? Is it to be read as poetry or drama? Does a
poetic text have an existence independent of the musical score? Do the words serve only as a dramatic framework for the composer? Must the text only be judged
as part of a musical score? The only cogent response to
these questions seems to be: it depends. No single measure of evaluation works in every case. Words play different roles in different operas. The text in Verdi and
Cammarano's *Il Trovatore* presents itself differently
than in Gilbert and Sullivan's *Trial by Jury*. Cammarano saw his mission as creating a scenario for explosive passion. Gilbert wanted the audience to hear and
react to every line. Cammarano worked for tears, Gilbert wanted smiles.

Different texts call different styles of operas into
existence. Maurice Maeterlinck's prose libretto for *Pelléas et Mélisande*, which contained no arias or ensem-

bles, would not have been an inspiring text for Puccini or Prokofiev, but it proved ideal for the slow and atmospheric music of Claude Debussy. What matters is the imaginative connection between the poet and musician. Part of a great opera composer's genius is the ability to find the right libretto. Johannes Brahms spent decades looking for the perfect text without success. He never composed the opera he so obsessively pondered. By contrast, Verdi always had some idea in the works and some librettist in his clutches, trying to create a text suited to his needs.

The general wisdom is generally true: the best test of a libretto is how well it operates in the finished work. But it is more accurate to rephrase the observation in a way that gives poets their due: the best test of a libretto is how effectively the words inspire the composer to create the finished work and the singers to perform it persuasively. As cultural historian Paul Robinson observed, "A libretto is not a text as we ordinarily understand that term." It can't be judged separately from the musical drama it inspires because its purpose is to create a *Gesamtkunstwerk*, an interdisciplinary work of art. A text for lyric drama looks different from a spoken play, but if its purpose is to inspire a composer to create "an interdisciplinary work of art," then its literary quality can't be unimportant. Composers who craft their own libretti do so with enormous care.

Wagner began his operas by composing his "poems." Only after the libretto was finished did the music come. The world premiere of *Der Ring des Nibelungen* was a marathon poetry reading in Zurich in 1852. It lasted two full days according to the composer's account. (Another source claims it spilled over into a third day.) Wagner demanded the audience's complete attention to his recitation. (He castigated a mother who left to nurse her sick child.) He enjoyed the performance so much that he read the poem again a few months later at the elegant Hotel Baur. This recitation filled four successive evenings. The composer considered his poem a finished work of art. He presented it to two audiences without music to be evaluated as a literary text.

As Wagner's example indicates, a text must have some independent literary force and value to be useful to a composer. A libretto is incomplete without music, but it isn't therefore negligible. The text exists in a state of potentiality; music will transform its meaning and merit. Viewed solely as a literary work, Boito's libretto for Verdi's *Otello*—although fine Italian verse—is inferior to Shakespeare's tragedy. Verdi's operatic setting, however, feels fully equal to Shakespeare's play; both are masterpieces of tragic drama. A libretto, therefore, cannot be judged on verbal quality isolated from the music. Opera's material essence is auditory, but words represent only a narrow part of that sonic dimension.

Yet doesn't the very idea of opera suggest a theatrical ambition beyond serviceable words set to music? The form was created to convey poetic drama through singing. There is no intrinsic reason why the words should be inferior to the music as long as they also fulfill their role in inspiring the music. Part of the thrill of popular musical theater comes from the lyrics, as any performance of *South Pacific*, *West Side Story*, or *Sweeney Todd* will demonstrate. Why does contemporary opera pretend otherwise? Opera has attracted major modern poets—including Brecht, Auden, Hofmannsthal, Gertrude Stein, Paul Claudel, Edna St. Vincent Millay, Langston Hughes, Gabriele D'Annunzio, Octavio Paz, and Guillaume Apollinaire. Some poets have written libretti that exist on the page as genuine literary works. Although such achievement is not mandatory, good poetry adds an imaginative frisson in musical drama that amplifies the work's expressive effect.

Our current standards for libretti are too low. Is it too much to hope that a new opera might have a book as good as a second-rate musical? At least the Broadway lyricists try to write their best. Why are most operatic poets slumming?

CHAPTER VIII

Auden Abandons Poetry

It never seems to happen that a poet sits down to write a libretto without first being commissioned.

—JAMES FENTON

GOOD POETRY DOESN'T HELP OPERA IF THE REST OF THE libretto lacks dramatic focus and narrative thrust. W. H. Auden's *Paul Bunyan* (1941) reads better than it performs—despite Benjamin Britten's inspired score—because the libretto succeeds more conspicuously as verse than drama. The zany ingenuity of Auden's lyrics complicates the action so consistently that the verbal energy highlights the libretto's inadequacy as theater. For example, midway in Act One, a "Quartet of the Defeated" enter and sing a brief ensemble. The lyrics do not aspire to poetry, but the quick quatrains work well as theatrical verse. Each character introduces himself with a striking first line, differentiating himself from the others before sharing his generic sob story:

TENOR SOLO

Gold in the North came the blizzard to say,
I left my sweetheart at the break of day,

The gold ran out and my love grew grey.
> You don't know all, sir, you don't know all.

BASS SOLO

The West, said the sun, for enterprise,
A bullet in Frisco put me wise,
My last words were, "God damn your eyes!"
> You don't know all, sir, you don't know all.

ALTO SOLO

In Alabama my heart was full,
Down to the river bank I stole,
The waters of grief went over my soul.
> You don't know all, sir, you don't know all.

BARITONE SOLO

In the streets of New York I was young and well
I rode the market, the market fell,
One morning I found myself in hell.
> I didn't know all, sir, I didn't know all.

ALL

> We didn't know all, sir, we didn't know all.

The problem is that these four characters, like many figures in *Paul Bunyan* (whose cast includes talking trees, geese, a dog, two cats, and an unseen giant lumberjack), serve no dramatic function. The quartet arrives, sings, and then disappears into the chorus. The libretto reads more like a pageant or parade than an opera. By comparison, Auden and Chester Kallman's texts for Hans Werner Henze's *Elegy for Young Lovers* (1961) and *The Bassarids* (1966) contain little significant poetry, but they work powerfully in performance as musical drama.

Elegy for Young Lovers presents an arresting realist drama about a devious and egotistic poet who manipulates the suffering of others to feed his art. The central character, the poet Gregor Mittenhofer, is an unflattering composite of W. B. Yeats and Rainer Maria Rilke, and the libretto reflects Auden's rejection of the Romantic notion that great artists transcend moral norms. *The Bassarids* is a vigorous adaptation of Euripides' *The Bacchae* that explores the psychosexual motives of the protagonist, King Pentheus. Subtly introducing ideas from Nietzsche and Freud into the tragedy, Auden and Kallman achieve masterful plotting and characterization. In both operas, the verse works well in its context, but little is independently memorable.

The difference between Auden's early and mature libretti cannot be accidental. If one reads his libretti in chronological order, one observes the authorial priority shifts from poetic considerations to dramatic ones. As Auden gained experience in opera, certainly influenced by Kallman, he made the lyrics secondary to characterization and plotting. The libretto for *Elegy for Young Lovers* has narrative power and psychological weight, but the clear and efficient verse calls little attention to itself. The implication of Auden's development is provocative. The most distinguished English-language librettist of the twentieth century eventually recognized that poetry could not animate opera unless it was incorporated into the other mostly nonverbal dramatic elements.

Another libretto that reads well on the page as verse drama is Ronald Duncan's much maligned text for Benjamin Britten's *The Rape of Lucretia* (1946). Freely based on a forgotten French play by André Obey, the opera depicts a famous episode in Roman history—the rape of a virtuous married woman by King Tarquin the Proud and her subsequent suicide. The incident so outraged Roman citizens that they overthrew the monarchy and established the Republic. The story has inspired work by many artists and writers, including Chaucer, Shakespeare, Botticelli, Titian, and Rembrandt. Duncan's libretto is poetically ambitious, dramatically intense, and theatrically innovative. It is no masterpiece, but it moves with surprising emotional and imaginative energy. Here the drunken general Junius complains that his comrade Collatinus's wife Lucretia has remained faithful while his own wife has made him a cuckold:

> Lucretia! Lucretia!
> I'm sick of that name.
> Her virtue is
> The measure of my shame.
> Now all of Rome
> Will laugh at me,
> Or what is worse

> Will pity me.
> Lucretia! Lucretia!
>
> Tomorrow the city urchins will sing my name to school,
> And call each other "Junius" inside of "fool."
> Collatinus will gain my fame with the Roman mob
> Not because of battles he has won
> —but because Lucretia's chaste
> —and the Romans being wanton worship chastity.
> Lucretia!

In theory, Duncan's libretto offered a level of complexity well suited to the intimacy of a chamber opera. In practice, it was too wordy and multi-layered for operatic theater. A student of F. R. Leavis and protégé of Ezra Pound, Duncan had played an important part—along with T. S. Eliot, Louis MacNeice, and Christopher Fry—in the British revival of verse drama after World War II. He had a successful career as a playwright, screenwriter, and translator.

The Rape of Lucretia was initially a critical success, but it failed financially when Britten toured the Modernist work through the provinces. Britten, who had composed a lyric but chromatic and astringent score, blamed his librettist. Duncan was dropped from the composer's inner circle and replaced by more ductile and conventional librettists for future projects. While the particular virtues of Duncan's florid text were not ideally suited to Britten's talents, the libretto remains a remarkable and original work. *The Rape of Lucretia* still holds a modest place in the international repertory, but no credit is given to Duncan. Britten's complaints have been taken at face value by posterity. In opera, such are the rewards of poetic independence and innovation. Only composers are praised for taking risks.

CHAPTER IX

Mozart vs. Mozart

*Pure image, comprehensible in a
pantomimic way—is what a good
opera libretto needs, for wholly a third
of the words nearly always get lost.*

—RICHARD STRAUSS

MOZART'S TWO FINAL OPERAS ARE *DIE ZAUBERFLÖTE*
(*The Magic Flute*) and *La Clemenza di Tito* (*The Clemency of Titus*). Although both works find the composer
at the height of his musical powers, *The Magic Flute* has
always been ranked as superior by both audiences and
critics. How can this consensus hold when *La Clemenza di Tito* contains magnificent music, and Metastasio's classical Italian verse is indisputably finer than
Emanuel Schikaneder's bumptious German doggerel?
Anyone who has seen both operas knows the answer:
The Magic Flute provides better theater.

However mediocre as a poet, Schikaneder was an
experienced man of the stage. Designing a star vehicle for his own comic talents, he planned the theatrical
effect of each scene. He created simple dramatic situations with strongly differentiated characters. He pep-

pered his scenes with clever sight gags. He even made
an irresistible love duet out of a stutter ("Pa-pa-pa-Pap-
pageno"). Schikaneder presented the narrative with the
pantomimic clarity Strauss claimed opera needed. As
Peggy Glanville-Hicks observed:

> A good opera is a good ballet story. If you can see who
> does what to which and what the result is, without under-
> standing a word of what they're singing, all to the good.

No one will praise Schikaneder for subtlety, but
his simple verse works effectively in its theatrical context. A libretto does not succeed on how well it reads
on the printed page. The words can only be judged in
their final context, set to music, supported by the pro-
saic virtues of the plot, character, and situation. Poetic
drama—comic or tragic—is not primarily poetic; it is
theater that uses poetry to intensify the language that
the drama requires. Schikaneder kept the action moving so smartly that the viewer overlooks the flaws in the
plot. His episodic structure allowed his comic antics to
alternate with elevated Masonic symbolism. The combination of high and low shouldn't work, but paradoxically the slapstick scenes give the Masonic rituals room
to resonate.

By contrast, Metastasio's carefully versified and
plotted libretto feels inert. Like *The Magic Flute*, *La
Clemenza di Tito* is an overtly moralistic work, but it
differs in genre. Metastasio wrote *La Clemenza* as an
opera seria, which portrays weighty matters in a noble

style and resolves the action in a happy ending. Consequently, *La Clemenza* makes its stately way, one gorgeous aria after another, not toward death or vengeance but clemency—not the most thrilling operatic climax. The poetry, elegant and elevated, slows rather than intensifies the drama. This beautiful but unlovable opera is rarely performed without substantial cuts. Ironically, Metastasio's *opera seria* delivers its moral lesson less convincingly than Schikaneder's farce, which frames its Masonic ideals in comedy and romance.

Not all artistic innovation is deliberate. Through a combination of poetic incompetence and theatrical intuition, Schikaneder unwittingly pointed to the future of the libretto. He mixed magic, love, and slapstick with elaborate quasi-religious ritual in ways that prefigure the spiritual ambitions of late Romantic operas such as *Die Meistersinger von Nürnberg* (*The Mastersinger of Nuremberg*) or *Die Frau ohne Schatten* (*The Woman Without a Shadow*). The homogenous nobility of classical *opera seria* was replaced with a more flexible and inclusive style. Meanwhile, as the size and instrumentation of the orchestra grew, the symphonic accompaniments took over much of the expressive task once conveyed by words. As the poetic elements became less important (and often less audible), the librettist strove to unify the works through myth and symbol.

CHAPTER X

Hofmannsthal Meets Strauss

Depth must be hidden. Where? On the surface.

—HUGO VON HOFMANNSTHAL

AT SEVENTEEN, HUGO VON HOFMANNSTHAL WAS ALREADY a famous poet across the German-speaking world—the literary *Wunderkind* of Vienna. By twenty-four, he had abandoned lyric poetry. He had stopped believing in the art's capacity to represent reality. He did not, however, stop writing verse. Distressed by the solipsism of modern poetry, Hofmannsthal turned to theater for its public and communal qualities. The realist drama then in vogue did not attract him. Like Yeats, he imagined a symbolic theater of myth and ritual similar to classical Greek or medieval drama. The poet's task, he felt, was to create "the myth of the time." He wrote well-regarded verse plays, but he aspired to the expressive power and stylized ritual of opera. Lyric poetry could be redeemed by returning to its ancient roots in song. "Words performed through music," he wrote, "can express what words alone had exhausted." Hofmannsthal sought out the most talented German-language opera composer, Richard Strauss. When the poet first offered his services, Strauss demurred, but once they worked together on adapting Sophocles' *Elektra*, the composer fell into the poet's thrall.

For the rest of his life Hofmannsthal collaborated with Strauss. Their partnership was an unlikely one. It resembled one of the royal marriages that characterized the Austro-Hungarian empire—not a love match but an astute strategic alliance. The elegant and aristocratic poet did not much like the coarse and uncultured Strauss, but he respected his musical genius. Together they created seven works (six operas and a ballet). At least four of the operas rank as acknowledged masterpieces, *Elektra* (1909), *Der Rosenkavalier* (1911), *Ariadne auf Naxos* (1912), and *Die Frau ohne Schatten* (1919). Their collaboration was unique in that each of these works was remarkably different from the others. Hofmannsthal shaped Strauss's operatic career as a series of dramatic experiments in different genres. No other operatic partnership equals it in terms of range and invention.

Elektra recreated the violent energy of classical tragedy sharpened by modern psychological insight. Strauss generated a huge orchestral sound that forced the singers to fight to be heard—a struggle that leaves an emotional impact on the audience. *Der Rosenkavalier* (*The Cavalier of the Rose*) offered an exquisite high-art version of operetta. Its charm and gaiety are deftly interlaced with gentle melancholy and bittersweet realism. The libretto endows each of the major characters with his or her personal style of speech, especially the

Marschallin. A great dramatist creates roles that allow great actors or singers to bring their full humanity into a character—Falstaff, Cyrano, Antigone, or Sonya (in Chekhov's *Uncle Vanya*). Hofmannsthal wrote such a part for his Marschallin, a beautiful but wistful aristocrat troubled by the onset of middle age, especially when in the company of her young lover. She is by turns playful, pensive, manipulative, and spoiled, but she is always self-possessed. One of the most nuanced characters in opera, the Marschallin has attracted some of the world's finest sopranos, including Lotte Lehman, Maria Reining, Elizabeth Schwarzkopf, Lisa Della Casa, Regine Crespin, Christa Ludwig, and Renée Fleming. Few operatic heroines express such quiet passion or speak with such intelligent candor. In one scene she muses over the mystery of time to the lover she is about to relinquish.

Die Zeit, die ist ein sonderbar Ding.
Wenn man so hinlebt, ist sie rein gar nichts.
Aber dann auf einmal.
Da spürt man nichts als sie:
Sie ist um uns herum, sie ist auch in uns drinnen.
In den Gesichtern rieselt sie, im Spiegel da rieselt sie.
In meinen Schläfen fließt sie.
Und zwischen mir und dir da fließt sie wieder,
Lautlos, wie eine Sanduhr.
Manchmal hör' ich sie fließen unaufhaltsam.
Manchmal steh' ich auf mitten in der Nacht
Und lass die Uhren alle, alle stehn.

[Time is a curious thing.
When you're just living, it's nothing at all.
But then suddenly,
one feels nothing else.
It's all around us, it's also inside us.
It trickles over faces, there in the mirror, it trickles,
it flows through my temples.
And between me and you, it flows as well,
Silent as an hourglass.
Sometimes I hear it flowing ceaselessly.
Sometimes I rise in the middle of the night
And stop all the clocks.]

Here Hofmannsthal uses *vers libre*, which alternates between blank verse and shorter or longer iambic lines, to give the Marschallin's monologue a formal but spontaneous feel. Her musings are both simple and sophisticated—the hushed melancholy of a convent girl whom time has transformed into an aging aristocrat. It is no wonder that the Viennese consider *Der Rosenkavalier* the opera that best captures their complicated character.

Ariadne auf Naxos (*Ariadne on Naxos*) presents an opera within an opera. The first half realistically depicts the preparations for a Viennese musical entertainment; the second half presents the mythic and comic presentation the guests see. *Ariadne auf Naxos* is a traditional and experimental opera in equal parts—a classical play ironized within a comic framework. Hofmannsthal mixes realism, myth, and *commedia dell'arte* into play-

ful Modernist metadrama. The results are simultaneously noble, farcical, and endearing. There is nothing
like it in the standard repertory.

Their next collaboration, *Die Frau ohne Schatten*,
delved into myth without the ironic detachment of *Ariadne* but with the raw energy of *Elektra*. *The Woman
Without a Shadow* pushes the genre of fairy tale opera
into the realm of primal myth. The opera centers on
the supernatural Empress who must obtain the shadow
of a mortal woman in order to have a child. If she fails
to conceive, her beloved husband, the Emperor, will
be turned into stone. She and her sinister Nurse convince the unhappy Dyer's Wife to trade her shadow for
luxuries and sensual pleasure. Hofmannsthal's Sym-
bolist drama portrays the crises and reconciliations of
the two troubled marriages. The tense and rapturous
drama explores sexual passion, marriage, and child-
bearing. The first two subjects are standard operatic
themes, the last becomes visionary in Hofmannsthal's
handling. In *Die Frau ohne Schatten*, children are the life
force that pulls humanity into the future. No modern
opera more powerfully develops the Wagnerian tradition of mythic music drama.

Hofmannsthal's two later libretti for Strauss produced less successful operas—*Die Ägyptische Helena*,
The Egyptian Helen (1928), and *Arabella* (1933). They
hold a minor place in the repertory on the strength of
the earlier works.

The Strauss and Hofmannsthal collaborations rank
among the most surprising and successful experiments

in modern opera. When Hofmannsthal died suddenly in 1929 at fifty-five, Strauss was left adrift. He set Hofmannsthal's *Arabella* to music posthumously. He then collaborated with Stefan Zweig on *Die Schweigsame Frau* (*The Silent Woman*), but Nazi Austria was no place for a Jewish writer. Zweig fled Vienna before the opera's 1935 premiere. For his next work, the composer ended up with Joseph Gregor, a theatrical scholar approved by the National Socialist party. A friend of Zweig, Gregor was no Nazi fanatic, just an academic opportunist of no particular talent. None of the four operas he wrote with Strauss rose to the level of the weakest Hofmannsthal work. The composer's final opera, *Capriccio* (1942), had a libretto by the conductor Clemens Krauss. The piece, which bears the subtitle "A Conversation with Music," has a bewitching score, but as musical theater, it is languid and evanescent. Perhaps escapist elegance was the most that could be accomplished in Nazi Germany.

Hofmannsthal's choice of drama as a corrective poetic medium both parallels and differs from the cases of Yeats and Eliot. The two poets underwent similar, though less extreme, artistic crises to Hofmannsthal's rejection of lyric verse. All three authors felt the elitist isolation of modern poetry and sought the communal power of theater. They prized poetic drama for its ritual qualities. Writing for actors and a physical audience anchored their imagination. Had Yeats and Eliot lived in Germany, they would have turned to opera. But in the early twentieth century, neither England nor Ireland offered opera as a possible alternative to spoken theater. Despite a few isolated experiments such as Gustav Holst's *Savitri* (1916), there was no modern tradition for English-language opera until Britten's *Peter Grimes* (1945) premiered two weeks after V-E Day. Its critical and popular success announced the new possibilities of British opera.

If the libretto adds constraints to the poet's imagination, it also offers the opportunity to tell stories outside the conventions of verisimilitude. In an era when Realism and Naturalism dominated spoken drama, music created a credible niche for fantasy, myth, and symbolism. The allegorical quality of Hofmannsthal's *Die Frau ohne Schatten* would have been risible without Strauss's monumental music animating the symbols. Jean Cocteau, Gertrude Stein, Bertolt Brecht, Guillaume Apollinaire, and Hofmannsthal all crafted theatrical experiments for the opera house that rejected realism. When Jean Cocteau wrote the libretto of *Oedipus Rex* for Igor Stravinsky, he had the text translated into Latin to give the drama a ritual grandeur not possible in vernacular theater. He then added a spoken French narrator who explains each scene in a way that further distances the action.

Apollinaire's Surrealist farce, *Les Mamelles de Tirésias* (*The Breasts of Tiresias*, 1917), seems silly and inconsequential as spoken theater. Francis Poulenc's joyful 1947 opera, however, weaves a sweet comic spell that gives the crazy characters a sad and fragile humanity. The action-packed opera is most famous for its opening scene. Therese, the *prima soprano*, announces that she is tired of her submissive life as a woman. She decides to become a man, and her breasts, depicted by two balloons, float away. She renames herself Tiresias and proceeds to conquer the world. Her husband, who has been forced to dress as a woman, ingeniously creates a baby-making machine that can produce 40,049 infants a day. He lives in ease since his quick-growing and talented children support him. The absurdist plot includes murders, resurrections, and a famine in Zanzibar. After many surreal adventures, the couple happily reunite. When the cast concludes the opera by walking to the footlights to sing, *"Cher public: faites des enfants!"* ("Dear audience: make babies!"), the lunacy is suffused by the memory of the 1.5 million French killed in the First World War (as well as the fresh horrors of a second war the battle-wounded Apollinaire did not live to see). The merry call for more children to provide more soldiers is opera's most surreal moment—absurd, horrifying, and, in Poulenc's setting, disturbingly charming. Music gives nonsense momentary substance and credibility. Opera can make even the oddest words sing.

CHAPTER XI

Opera as Primitive Spectacle

*Composers should throw out
most of their words.*

—JOAQUÍN NIN-CULMELL

OPERA DEMANDS EXTREME NARRATIVE COMPRESSION.
It cannot present complex plotting as easily as film or
fiction. While the structure of opera is narrative, its
driving energy is lyric; it lacks the novel's ability to
communicate the duration of time. Opera excels at por-
traying peak moments of human emotion. Better perhaps than any other narrative form, it projects the full
emotional intensity of a significant moment from the
perspective of a particular character. It can also convey
the simultaneous feelings of multiple personalities in
duets, trios, or larger ensembles. Masterfully done, such
ensembles create a dizzying effect. Opera's lyric fer-
vency explains why people often cry at performances,
even at works they have known for years. For a few
moments they merge into the character on the stage.
The imaginary figure's suffering evokes their own.

There is something archaic, even primitive, about
the spectacle of people chanting their joys and sorrows

from a stage—their voices filling large halls without electronic amplification. That strange remoteness increases when the work is performed in a foreign language. Ritual, not realism, is evidently the goal—but to what purpose? The elaborate pageantry and stylized acting recall the form's earliest ambition to replicate ancient tragedy, an art that was equally sacred and civic. Opera became a secular ritual to summon and confront the audience's sorrows and desires.

Composers and librettists have understood that this emotional transference is essential to opera's identity. "Opera cuts to the chase as death does," said Julian Barnes. "It is an art that seeks, more obviously than any other form to break your heart." The librettist arranges the dramatic action to move from one emotional episode to another, always leading to passionate new climaxes. Amplitude, balance, verisimilitude, and subtlety may be virtues in a novel, but they hardly matter in a libretto. Opera strives for lyrical beauty, dramatic situations, and emotional intensity. If the novel tends to investigate the meaning of quotidian existence, opera explores the extremes of human experience, especially the outmost limits of suffering. The singers must weep, shudder, and die.

Tragic opera remains the only theatrical form still unabashedly committed to Aristotle's notion of emotional catharsis through pity and terror. Twentieth century literary critics lamented "The Death of Tragedy." They declared that tragic theater had declined after the generation of Goethe and Schiller because as *literary* critics they looked only at spoken theater. The nineteenth century, however, was one of tragedy's greatest periods—equaled only by Periclean Athens or Elizabethan London. The great tragedies of the Romantic age did not appear on the theatrical stage but in the opera house. The masterpieces were not written by Shelley, Byron, Hugo, or Hölderlin; they were composed by Bellini, Donizetti, Verdi, and Wagner.

Although opera is mostly lyric in its effect, those heightened moments require narrative and psychological context to work their enchantments. The text must be judged less for its verbal felicity than the depth of its characterization and memorability of its dramatic situations. Psychology is not a concern that most poets bring to their verse; but in creating a compelling libretto, a gift for psychological portrayal is as necessary as facility in versification. Not meter nor metaphor, but motive and melody drive opera.

Opera libretti are often criticized for their sudden shifts of plot. To the novelist, operatic narrative seems fragmented and insufficient. The genius of the Italian libretto rests on its passionate adherence to a simple dramatic principle—the audience does not need to be told everything. A few evocative details can trigger a scene's full emotive and imaginative impact. In a manner reminiscent of Modernist poetry, Italian libretti achieve their effects as much by what they omit as what they include.

The necessary compression of a good libretto explains why operatic plots appear disjunctive and hyperbolic to a reader accustomed to prose fiction. Felice Romani sought different effects than did his contemporary, Jane Austen. Opera requires emotional clarity and immediacy, not the meticulous examination of motivation, sensibility, and social context that enliven the novel. Most English-language literati, unfamiliar with opera in performance and generally unable to read libretti in the original language, misunderstand the aesthetic of opera—intellectually and experientially. "The Englishman is musical," declared George Bernard Shaw, "but he is not operatic." If traditional literati approve of any opera at all, like Shaw, they prefer Wagner's *Ring*, which takes four evenings to unfold. It is the only opera that moves as slowly as a novel. Wagner has many virtues, but they do not include compression.

CHAPTER XII

Verse or Prose?

*That Romani! He promises everything
but hands over nothing.*

—GAETANO DONIZETTI

THE CHALLENGE FOR THE CONTEMPORARY COMPOSER IS to find a collaborator with the skills necessary to create a compelling libretto. Two hundred years ago there were poets who specialized in writing theatrical verse, especially for the prestigious medium of opera. Today there is no living literary tradition of writing libretti. Nor is there much expertise among the management of opera companies in evaluating texts beyond checking that they deliver the bare theatrical essentials.

The first question a composer asks today would never have occurred to Verdi or Wagner—should the libretto be in prose or verse? Is poetry still the right medium for opera? Wouldn't prose be a more direct and natural medium? What sort of writer brings more to the project—the poet or the playwright? That is a harder question to answer than it should be. Today's poets have little experience in writing for the stage or composing lyrics for music. Playwrights understand dramatic structure and characterization, but they lack experience in the extreme compression and lyric language opera requires. Contemporary spoken theater is all prose; the plots are mostly talk-driven with little on-stage action. Much of the drama isn't even in the dialogue but in the subtext, the important things that go unsaid. Opera requires a greater degree of direct emotion and visible action.

A common mistake of contemporary composers has been to set prose plays to music. They take the script and cut it down to a fraction of its original size. Too often the results are familiar plots and naturalistic language submerged in atmospheric background music. There is too much dialogue and too few powerful lyric moments. A fabulous play is no guarantee of a compelling opera. The pacing and procedures of spoken theater have little relation to the spellcasting and lyric abandon required of opera. André Previn's *A Streetcar Named Desire* (1995), for example, meanders through hours of musical conversation while the audience waits for the real singing to begin. The score is tasteful, intelligent, and lifeless. Mina Loy said, "Poetry is prose bewitched." Enchantment is also the goal of opera, and it is naïve to assume that the composer brings all of the magic.

When William Bolcom adapted Arthur Miller's *A View from the Bridge* (1999) for opera, the playwright worked with the composer's long-time collaborator Arnold Weinstein to add some lyrics. Their adaptation—Miller's prose with some short verse passages—

was so respectful that the final work felt less operatic than the original play. Given the brilliance of the cabaret songs Bolcom and Weinstein had written together, one wonders if Miller's play should not have been entirely recast as verse. Miller's prose was too tough to be subdued. As the reviewer in *Gramophone* noted about the recording, "Why does one sit through it with the unsettling feeling that the music is somehow superfluous?" "So many of these new operas—by words possessed!" bemoaned Cuban American composer Joaquín Nin-Culmell who claimed that libretti need extreme concision to achieve the necessary "operatic speed."

William Butler Yeats considered the question of lyric intensity in the early twentieth century when he sought to revive poetic drama—a venture he felt needed to incorporate music and dance. What did Yeats believe poetic imagination brought to modern theater?

> It is not very difficult to construct a fairly vigorous prose play, and then . . . decorate it and encumber it with poetry. But a play of that kind will never move us poetically, because it does not uncover, as it were, that high, intellectual, delicately organized soul of men and of an action, that may not speak aloud if it does not speak in verse.

Should composers write their own libretti? Enough musicians have managed the task to demonstrate the virtues of single authorship. Berlioz, Donizetti, Leoncavallo, Boito, Prokofiev, Menotti, and Wagner all wrote the words for operas that posterity prizes. Boito was a writer and composer in equal parts. Prokofiev wrote or co-authored his libretti. A less well-known example is Donizetti, not a literary man, who had a talent for comedy. He wrote hilarious libretti for *Le Convenienze Teatrali*, *Il Campanello*, and co-authored *Don Pasquale*, a comic masterpiece. Donizetti knew his own limitations: he left the creation of his tragic libretti to poets.

The double role of composer-poet doesn't always go well. With Hector Berlioz, the dangers of single authorship became apparent. A capable poet, he had no gift for dramatic compression. Composers often tell librettists what to cut. The editorial task becomes harder when the composers judge their own verse. Berlioz's grand opera *Les Troyens* (1858), based on Virgil's *Aeneid*, grew too long and complex to be staged. The five-act epic staggers under the weight of its own magnificence. For years producers cut it into two pieces to stage—*La prise de Troie* (*The Fall of Troy*) and *Les Troyens à Carthage* (*The Trojans at Carthage*). The first complete performance did not occur until twenty years after the composer's death. The great work remains a specialty item.

The literary problems of libretti written by composers go beyond epic length. Some composers create sheer chaos—Olympian ineptitude in plotting, characterization, dialogue, and versification. British composer Michael Tippett wrote intellectually ambitious and hopelessly jumbled libretti. Allusive, mythic, and symbolic psychodramas, they are ill-suited for lyric theater. Tippett's best opera, *The Midsummer Marriage*

(1955), boasts a gorgeously distinctive score, but the text is so confusing that the work is dramatically incoherent. The convoluted plot involves two lovers surrounded by assorted symbolic characters who range from a mechanic to an ancient She-Priestess and two figures borrowed from T. S. Eliot's *The Waste Land*. The composer had tried to convince T. S. Eliot to write the text, but Old Possum slyly suggested that Tippett write his own libretto. The opera survives on the margins of the repertory solely on its musical merit.

Most composers lack the literary skill to write their own words, and they know it. The issue is not whether to collaborate but how to do so effectively. An extended partnership of complementary artists seems the ideal situation in opera—if the right partners can be joined. So many enduring works in the international repertory are products of so few partnerships that stable creative collaboration clearly has decisive benefits. The operatic ideal is not simply a matter of getting a skilled librettist and composer together; it also requires sustaining a collaboration that satisfies and challenges both artists. One saw the power of such partnerships in the operas created by John Adams and Alice Goodman—*Nixon in China* (1972) and *The Death of Klinghoffer* (1991). When Adams dropped Goodman for libretti by the director Peter Sellars, the quality of his work suffered. Sellars is not a writer. He understands theatrical effect, but he has no gift for characterizations, plotting, or dramatic coherence. Adams has never written another opera to equal his first two.

A sadder testament to the power of partnership comes when the librettist or lyricist dies. After Hofmannsthal's death, Strauss never wrote another major opera. Broadway offers similar stories of partnership and loss. Lyricist Jerry Ross and composer Richard Adler created two hit musicals, *Pajama Game* (1954) and *Damn Yankees* (1955). Both shows won the Tony. Ross died suddenly at twenty-four. Adler continued to compose for half a century without creating another significant theatrical work.

CHAPTER XIII

A Tale of Two Composers

*At best, an artist can find a certain kind
of serenity in resigning himself
to the curse of imperfection.*

—GIAN CARLO MENOTTI

THE ADVANTAGES AND DISADVANTAGES OF SINGLE AUTHOR-
ship are illustrated in the careers of two mid-twentieth-
century American composers—Gian Carlo Menotti
and Carlisle Floyd. The Italian-born Menotti and South
Carolinian Floyd make an unlikely pair, but they share
several unusual qualities. Both men wrote all of their
own libretti. Both composed tonal music that ignored
Modernist trends. Both achieved exceptional early success. They even shared longevity. Both men died at 95
after long, fortunate, and—this will be my subject—
artistically disappointing lives.

Menotti had an extraordinary career that spanned
seven decades. He composed twenty-five operas. For
years he was the most widely performed living operatic
composer in the world. He brought five of his works
to Broadway for commercial runs—four hits and one
flop—a record no other classical composer is likely

to match. Not only did he earn two Pulitzer Prizes in music, in 1955 his opera *The Saint of Bleecker Street* won both the New York Drama Critics' Circle Award for best musical and New York Music Critics' Circle Award for best opera.

The most famous moment in Menotti's life, however, had come a few years earlier. On Christmas Eve, 1951, NBC broadcast the world premiere of his one-act Christmas opera, *Amahl and the Night Visitors*, as part of Hallmark's primetime Hall of Fame series. It was the first opera ever commissioned for American television. Broadcast live, coast to coast, on 35 NBC affiliates, it reached five million viewers, the largest audience for any opera performance in history—not only then but probably even now. A successful Met simulcast on PBS rarely reaches more than 700,000 households, even though the U.S. population has doubled since *Amahl*'s premiere.

Menotti's elegant and tender opera about a crippled boy who meets the Three Magi on their way to Bethlehem, created a national sensation. Olin Downes reviewed it on the front page of the *New York Times* as "always poetic and atmospheric . . . never obvious or banal." The short opera, he declared, was an "historical event in the rapidly evolving art of television." Christmas broadcasts of *Amahl* became annual events, but the opera's appeal wasn't confined to television. Conceived for the small stage of live television, the opera could easily be mounted by regional companies, colleges, and amateur groups. It soon became the most widely produced opera in the world. (Nearly two decades later in 1969, there were still 350 productions in the U.S. alone.) Menotti had been a well-known composer from the start. *Amahl* made the forty-year-old Italian émigré the chief figure of American opera.

Menotti also kept himself visible and relevant by creating two major international arts festivals—the Festival of the Two Worlds in Spoleto, Italy and the Spoleto Festival USA in Charleston, South Carolina. The composer had both a soft Italian charm and the keen Italian passion for quarrels. He made headlines for his arguments with the management of his festivals—usually followed by his public resignation, backroom negotiations, and triumphant return. Even Menotti's personal life seemed favored by the gods. Handsome and gregarious, he knew everyone from Arturo Toscanini to Jackie Kennedy. His lifelong partner was the composer Samuel Barber. The two had met as teenagers when Menotti came to America to study at the Curtis Institute in Philadelphia. Even after Menotti ended their romantic relationship in 1970, the two men remained intimate friends. (The break-up was largely due to Barber's depression and alcoholism aggravated by the catastrophic premiere of his *Antony and Cleopatra* at the opening of the new Metropolitan Opera House.) By the time Barber died in 1981, Menotti had relocated to Europe. He spent his final years commuting between his festivals or residing in Yester House, a Palladian manor in Scotland. Has any opera composer ever led a more active or gratifying life?

No one ever listed Menotti among the great composers of his time. His operas worked persuasively in
performance, but his effective and efficient scores faded
as one left the theater. His music lacked a strong individual profile. As most composers do, Menotti synthe-
sized a style rather than invented one, but he handled
his fabricated idiom with agility and confidence. His
works have fluency, coherence, and striking economy.
With the exception of *The Consul*, all of his best operas
are short, each under an hour. Menotti's music had a
generic Italian sound rooted in the *verismo* composers—Puccini, Mascagni, and Leoncavallo—to which he
added touches of modern French orchestral color and
lively Broadway pacing.

Menotti is often depicted as a musical reactionary,
but it is more accurate to consider him a latecomer—
the last Italian operatic composer to reach an international audience. Italian opera was still a vibrant
tradition when Menotti was born in 1911. Puccini had
just premiered *La Fanciulla del West* (1910) at the Metropolitan Opera, and his last five operas were still to
come—*La Rondine* (1917), the three one-act works of
Il Trittico (1918), which also premiered at the Met (*Il
Tabarro, Suor Angelica*, and *Gianni Schicchi*), and finally
Turandot (1926). There was still international demand
for new Italian operas. Italo Montemezzi's *L'Amore dei
Tre Re* (*The Love of Three Kings*) opened in Milan in 1913
and moved the next year to the Met, Covent Garden,
and other companies. Montemezzi soon came to America, married an heiress, and spent the rest of his life

managing his career in both countries. No fan of Mussolini, he sat out World War II in a mansion in Beverly Hills, California.

For the young Menotti, Italian opera seemed very much alive, and its future involved the United States. The death of his father led him to America, though he never changed his Italian citizenship. When the Met mounted its first Menotti opera, *Amelia Goes to the Ball*, in 1938, the twenty-six-year-old composer would have seen himself in a living lineage. Who would have thought that after three and a half centuries of sustained creativity and innovation, Italian opera would cease to produce new works that commanded international attention? Most of the *verismo* masters were still alive—Mascagni, Giordano, Montemezzi, Riccardo Zandonai, and Francesco Cilea. Menotti seemed to be the first member of a new generation. As it turned out, that generation never arrived on the international scene.

Critical praise for Menotti always seemed to come with some reservation—not so much for what he had done as what he had not done. His best operas were excellent but never masterpieces. Yet no one could deny his obvious achievement. For the first time since George Gershwin, an American composer had written popular opera—not just one but half a dozen. As Ned Rorem observed, "Menotti single-handedly revitalized the concept of living opera in the United States." As it turned out, that accomplishment wasn't enough.

As a composer, Menotti was consigned to the bittersweet status described by Somerset Maugham to characterize his own fiction—"in the first rank of the second rate." Maugham's self-deprecating remark is no insult. Although he did not count himself among the great masters, Maugham also knew his work was likely to survive. His masterfully told novels remain popular, if not particularly fashionable; the same is true for Menotti's best operas.

Menotti possessed a natural gift for lyric theater with none of the awkward self-consciousness that inhibited most American composers of his era. He instinctively understood something his Modernist contemporaries had forgotten: opera is a celebration of the human voice. Much of what opera communicates does not come from the musical score but the bodies that convey it. The expressive sounds formed in the lungs, larynx, and throats of singers make a primal physical connection with the listener. The human voice transforms abstract notes into visceral emotion—not just onstage but inside the bodies of the audience. The insight was not original to Menotti; it was the central impulse of Italian opera. His achievement was to recreate the traditional magic in English in works that attracted millions of listeners.

How can such a career be called disappointing? It is no small thing to make the first rank of the second rate. To be only a cherub and not a seraph is still a form of immortality. Just ask the seven lower choirs of angels. Not everyone can be Mozart or Verdi. No Italian composer since Puccini accomplished more than Menotti. (And no Italian American composer has come close.)

Menotti's heyday has passed, but a few works survive in the repertory along with a handful of operas by other minor masters from the generation of Mascagni and Giordano.

The true problem with Menotti's career is not his honorable secondary status but the bewildering collapse of his creative instincts at the height of his success. Despite a working life of over sixty years, Menotti wrote all of his best operas in the decade after World War II—*The Medium* (1946), *The Telephone* (1947), *The Consul* (1950), and *Amahl and the Night Visitors* (1951). To the short list, one should add his most original theatrical work, *The Unicorn, the Gorgon, and the Manticore* (1956), "a madrigal fable" for chorus, dancers, and chamber orchestra. Eighteen operas followed *Amahl*. None has held even a minor place in the repertory. After its remarkable start, Menotti's work never deepened or developed.

Carlisle Floyd had a similar though smaller career. Born and raised in the American South, Floyd was a twenty-eight-year-old professor in Tallahassee when his first full-length opera, *Susannah* (1955), premiered at Florida State. Retelling the story of Susannah and the Elders from the Book of Daniel, Floyd set his libretto in rural Tennessee. His tuneful and accessible score had a folkloric quality that seemed to grow naturally out of his opera's Appalachian setting. Direct, lyric, and theatrical, *Susannah* was an immediate success. His young backwoods heroine, Susannah Polk, had the compelling dramatic presence of a classic soprano role as did her nemesis, the pious but lecherous Reverend Olin Blitch. *Susannah* was not just a milestone for Florida State; the American South had never hosted such an operatic premiere.

One year later the New York City Opera staged *Susannah* to general acclaim. Both critics and audiences saw it as key work in a new movement of populist American opera. Two years later the New York production was brought to the Brussels World Fair (which also featured a Menotti world premiere). The popularity of Floyd's debut work has never wavered.

Susannah arrived just as the regional opera movement gained momentum in the United States. New companies emerged in Santa Fe, Seattle, Kansas City, Minneapolis, Philadelphia, Houston, St. Louis, and other cities. Even philistine Washington, D.C. launched a fledgling company. Those large municipal institutions were only part of a larger trend. As Menotti remarked, "Now, all of a sudden, every college and every university has an opera theater. Every little city has its little group."

In this new musical landscape *Susannah* gradually became the most frequently produced American opera after Gershwin's *Porgy and Bess*. Singers loved the roles, all so diatonic, demotic, and dramatic. There were no tone rows to memorize or angular vocal lines to navigate. All a singer had to do was to master a Tennessee accent. It is hard to attend any American vocal competition without hearing Susannah's radiant opening aria, "Ain't it a Pretty Night?" Sopranos learn it in school and dream of singing it on stage.

Floyd wrote ten more operas, including *Wuthering Heights* (1958), *The Passion of Jonathan Wade* (1962), *Markheim* (1966), *Of Mice and Men* (1970), *Willie Stark* (1981), and *Cold Sassy Tree* (2000). None achieved lasting success, though *Of Mice and Men* is occasionally revived. Floyd continued to be an influential figure in American opera. The courtly Southerner flourished as a symbol of the vanishing populist tradition in classical music. He served as composer-in-residence at Houston Grand Opera, which premiered, revived, recorded, and televised his work. Floyd was an inspirational figure, especially in the South; he proved that a composer didn't have to move to New York or Los Angeles to make a mark.

Menotti and Floyd helped establish the dominant mid-century style of American opera—resolutely tonal and emotionally direct music with realistic libretti depicting the struggles and obsessions of ordinary lives. The new operatic aesthetic became a conservative alternative to the progressive mainstream of American classical music that was incorporating European Modernism. The regional opera world insulated itself in a sort of parallel universe—the last refuge of big tunes and graceful vocal lines. The only acknowledgment of the Second Viennese School came when Menotti used twelve-tone music for parody.

The mid-century American operatic style is often called neo-Romantic, but that description is misleading. "Neo-Romantic" was the period's code word for contemporary music that was not atonal or experimental.

The mid-century style was melodic and dramatic in the traditional manner, but it was more restrained than late European Romanticism. No one would confuse Douglas Moore's popular *The Ballad of Baby Doe* (1956) with Erich Wolfgang Korngold's *Die Tote Stadt* (1920). Both are tragic operas about love and obsession. Korngold's music is rapturous and lush; the singers vacillate between emotional extremes. *The Ballad of Baby Doe*, which has a libretto by Broadway lyricist John Latouche, is a well-paced melodrama which could have been a major studio film. Moore's eclectic score was an accessible mix of operatic, theatrical, and folk styles. Compared to Korngold's feverish opera about necrophilia, Moore's depiction of a doomed romantic triangle in a Colorado mining town feels like an operetta.

For the regional opera companies and their new audiences, populism was the style of choice—an American sound, classical but democratic, and not too far from Broadway. Operas continued to be written in more challenging styles, such as Hugo Weisgall's *Six Characters in Search of an Author* (1959), Lou Harrison's *Rapunzel* (1959), and Roger Sessions's *Montezuma* (1964), but they had few productions. Sessions had to premiere his opera in Berlin. Until the rise of Philip Glass and the Minimalists in the 1980s, the populist school of Floyd, Menotti, and Moore held sway in America's opera houses.

Despite the public success of Menotti and Floyd and their undeniable impact on American opera, a sense of artistic failure haunts their reputations. Their marginalization has little to do with their musical conservatism, though that doesn't help. The perplexing issue is that neither composer realized his early promise nor meaningfully developed his artistic gift. For both men, their earliest operas were their best. By their early forties, both composers were stuck in a simple idiom they could neither escape nor keep vital. They received many commissions and much institutional support. Yet neither composer wrote an enduring opera in the last fifty years of his career.

This observation is not designed to belittle the achievements of either Menotti or Floyd. My goal has been to assess their careers accurately. To compose one opera that outlives its creator is a rare accomplishment. How many American operas from the first half of the twentieth century survive today? No more than half a dozen, most of which were written by Menotti. Nonetheless, a half century slump is hard to ignore. What went wrong?

Single authorship was a challenge that both men surmounted in their early work. It gave their first operas a seamless quality. But as their careers progressed, writing their own libretti may have undermined their creative growth. Menotti and Floyd were accomplished vocal composers but only serviceable writers. Their streamlined plots and conventional characters gave their early operas an appealing simplicity, but their words never rose to the evocative level of the music. Simplicity and sincerity are powerful artistic qualities, but they are difficult to sustain. They harden over time into a practiced and predictable manner.

Each composer chose a different literary strategy for their later operas. Neither approach worked well. Menotti continued to develop original plots. His works grew longer and more ambitious. *The Saint of Bleecker Street*, *The Last Savage*, *Goya*, and *La Loca* all strived for epic resonance. They were misjudgments of Menotti's modest talent. Their larger scope had the unintended effect of amplifying their literary defects—sentimental plots, banal dialogue, and inconsequential lyrics. Floyd sought the safety of adapting established works. He wrote libretti based on *Wuthering Heights*, *Of Mice and Men*, *Cold Sassy Tree*, and *All the King's Men*. Adaptation requires a special literary skill, the ability to make the borrowed characters and situations seem fresh and new. Floyd's later operas had the second-hand feeling—solid musical settings that never come fully alive in operatic terms. They leaned too heavily on their sources for effect. Worse yet, the texts lacked the poetic moments that would have inspired the memorable lyric passages that enlivened *Susannah*.

Consider the challenge of single authorship. Writing an opera is not as simple as writing a song. Operas are long and complicated. One must compose hours of music for multiple voices and orchestra. The text must create distinctive characters and arresting dramatic events, all conveyed with compression, lyricality, and coherence. To manage this feat once or twice is remarkable. In the history of opera, only one composer, Richard Wagner, sustained a major career writing all of his own words and music.

Wagner could spend years laboring over a "poem," which is how he referred to a libretto. He knew that the music had to grow organically from its lines. His writing and music evolved together. The slow and expansive pace of Wagner's late operas, which allowed the composer to enthrall the listener and build to overpowering climaxes, would have been impossible without verse designed to support the music's cumulative effect.

To read Wagner's libretti in chronological order is to see the continuous development of a great writer. Although rarely viewed from a purely literary perspective, Wagner was Germany's major poetic dramatist of the nineteenth century. Among librettists, only Metastasio and Hofmannsthal show comparable artistic range and growth, but neither wrote music. Wagner's achievement is incomparable. He created a series of operatic masterpieces, each with its own musical and dramatic personalities, culminating in his four-part *Der Ring des Nibelungen* (1869–1876), which ranks with Goethe's two-part *Faust* as the two greatest works of German drama. There are many examples of how an exceptional libretto can inspire a composer to create a single work of exceptional quality. Wagner's career demonstrates how treating every libretto as seriously as the music escalates a composer's artistic growth.

In comparison with Wagner's dynamism, Menotti and Floyd's careers seem obstructed. By early middle age—the point where most artists reach their prime—they were trapped in their own creative procedures. Their operatic styles had never been particularly original, but now their approach had lost its freshness. They prized creative control; but writing their own libretti divided their energy without stimulating their creativity. Neither composer could craft words or characters that surprised them. An opera can't go anywhere its libretto doesn't suggest.

"Great genius takes shape," Heinrich Heine wrote, "by contact with another great genius, but less by assimilation than friction." The history of musical theater demonstrates how often the arrival of a new librettist, such as Da Ponte, Boito, Hofmannsthal, or Hammerstein, transformed and elevated a composer's work. Neither Floyd nor Menotti ever had the stimulus of another strong imagination to lead or provoke them into new territory. They wrote the texts they already knew how to set, and their professional stature meant they never had to worry about finding someone to stage them. (In Menotti's case, he staged his own works at his festivals.) One wonders if their creative torpor couldn't have been solved with a simple action—hiring a poet or playwright as librettist.

My thesis is speculative and therefore unprovable. There are other possible explanations for their decline. Perhaps neither composer had the inner drive to realize his full talent. Perhaps their populist aesthetic left them too little room to grow. Maybe they were too distracted by other events—personal or professional. Menotti's festivals occupied much of his time and energy. Maybe all of these things are true.

Nonetheless the refusal of these composers to give

up single authorship and seek collaborators seems a compelling diagnosis. It fits the facts and addresses the central problem in these composer's careers. There are many ways in which promising young artists go wrong. Creativity at the highest level is hard to achieve and harder to sustain and enlarge. Sometimes even a genius needs help.

CHAPTER XIV

Searching for a Tradition

Verse should have two obligations:
to communicate a precise instance
and to touch us physically,
as the presence of the sea does.

—JORGE LUIS BORGES

WHY SPEND SO MUCH TIME ON THE TRUNCATED CAREERS
of two minor modern composers? Neither artist figures prominently in current cultural consciousness.
Wouldn't it have been more useful to have devoted
the previous chapter to Richard Wagner, a composer
of historic literary accomplishment? His operas not
only achieved a remarkable unity of words and music
but also demonstrated continuous artistic growth. Yes,
Wagner would have shown the possibilities of single authorship better than the mid-career impasses of
Floyd and Menotti. I can't dispute the objection. I could
plead exculpatory circumstances; there are already two
thousand books about Wagner.

But that's not the reason I brooded over Menotti
and Floyd. Their failures feel more relevant than Wagner's unprecedented series of triumphs. Menotti and

Floyd were American composers, and I am an American poet who writes libretti. Their troubled careers intrigue me because they provide perspective on my own situation. I work in an operatic tradition in which the poet has no defined place, a theatrical system which gives the libretto no respect, and a musical culture in which opera has only a marginal position.

I have been fascinated with modern classical music since my teenage years. When my classmates were buying albums by Jimi Hendrix, Cream, and the Byrds, I borrowed their records so I could spend my money on Stravinsky, Hindemith, Poulenc, and Britten. I bought the few contemporary American operas that were available, such as Barber's *Vanessa*, Bernstein's *Trouble in Tahiti*, or Copland's *The Tender Land*. I was lucky to have a high school friend who shared my passion for music and literature. Jim Laffan played trumpet. I played clarinet. He played piano brilliantly; I played piano. We explored music together. I had a vague dream of being a composer.

Fifty years ago, it was difficult to hear contemporary classical music, especially opera. Today the internet has created a cultural economy of unmanageable abundance. Nearly everything is one click away—available anywhere you can get a digital signal. A listener is no longer dependent on record companies or commercial media. Technology has allowed musicians to record and share their own performances. There is more music available on my cellphone than there was at the Stanford Music Library during my undergraduate years.

I grew up in a culture of scarcity. The shortage was especially keen in my rough-edged hometown in which the only cultural institution was the public library. There was no live music, theater, or visual art. The problem wasn't merely finding the arts; we didn't even know what to look for. There was no one to talk to, no older person who knew about these things to advise us. It took effort to hear new music, see a play, or find an unusual book. These difficulties, however, had an advantage. It made us value each encounter. As economics avows, scarcity increases value.

The problem wasn't just the lack of a global distribution system such as YouTube. Back in the sixties little modern American music had been recorded, and less still had been released on commercial labels. The few pieces that made it to vinyl usually went out of print. Contemporary music was seldom broadcast on the radio. Orchestras and opera companies did not perform as many new works as they do today. We attended performances at colleges and conservatories. We searched for out-of-print recordings in used record stores. We found piano scores to work through on our own. Music didn't come to us. We hunted for it. Searching was part of the experience.

I had one cultural advantage. I owned a 1955 Ford Fairlane, which I had bought for $100. Gas was twenty cents a gallon. Jim and I drove all over Southern California, which is admittedly something teenage boys don't mind doing, to attend free concerts and performances. It was the age of high print-culture, each Sunday the *Los Angeles Times* listed every forthcoming concert in Southern California. Any concert within a hundred-mile radius was fair game.

Wordsworth and Coleridge talked about poetry and philosophy as they hiked the mountain paths of the Lake District. Jim and I had the San Diego and Harbor Freeways for our wandering. We discussed literature and music for hours as we drove to our distant destinations. My comparison is comic but only partially so. Young artists can only begin where they find themselves, be it late eighteenth-century Cumbria or mid-twentieth-century Los Angeles. Exploring and talking is what young artists do. They need to experience as much art as possible and then assimilate it by asserting, arguing, and revising their opinions. It is a brand of education, different from sitting in a classroom, and it is the best way to discover and develop individual taste. Oscar Wilde observed, "It is only an auctioneer who can equally and impartially admire all schools of art." The rest of us have special insights, passionate loves, tenacious antipathies, and blind spots. To assume otherwise is a delusion. Some people have better taste than others, but no one's taste is infallible. The important thing is to feel one's true response and not subsist on a diet of second-hand opinions.

As a teenager, I saw a remarkable number of modern operas, mostly for free—*The Love for Three Oranges, The Bassarids, The Rape of Lucretia, Die Kluge, La Voix Humaine, The Crucible, Amahl and the Night Visitors, Albert Herring, Dialogues of the Carmelites,* and *Bomarzo.*

95

I came to know opera without academic supervision. I liked *The Bassarids* so much, I went back to USC the next evening to hear it again. After all, it was free. (It was performed in English with its superb Auden-Kallman libretto.) I listened to the weird "world premiere" of Bernard Hermann's *Wuthering Heights*—the composer's self-produced recording was played on a local radio station. Hermann said a few words—perhaps by phone—and the announcer played the entire work. I bought the expensive box set of Hermann's opera to support the project. I have hardly listened to it over the past half century—*Wuthering Heights* is a disappointing work—but when I see the old album, I still feel the frisson of its invisible premiere on my bedroom radio. Even disappointment can be sweet.

I've stayed engaged with contemporary music. As an adult, I've attended every production of modern opera I could manage. I have two walls full of opera recordings, especially modern works. For several years I worked as a classical music critic for *San Francisco Magazine*. During my six years at the helm of the National Endowment for the Arts, I helped fund dozens of world premieres and revivals. In early middle age my involvement became more personal. Although I had long ago given up my notion of being a composer, I now began writing texts for composers. As a librettist, I've added five operas to the tradition. American opera is something I have heard, seen, and thought about. I have concluded that it is a puzzling and thwarted enterprise—as befuddled as current American poetry but with a bigger budget.

In Germany, Italy, or Russia, opera is not merely part of the national musical culture; it represents part of the national identity. Italians can't discuss the unification of Italy without mentioning Verdi. Wagner looms over modern German culture like a failed god. In America, opera plays no part in shaping cultural consciousness. Broadway and Hollywood created our lyric theater. Disney's *The Little Mermaid* has more cultural presence than all of the operas of Menotti, Floyd, Barber, and Copland combined. It is no coincidence that the most successful American opera, *Porgy and Bess*, premiered on Broadway and unfolds mostly by the theatrical conventions of the popular musical. It belongs to the history of Broadway as much as to classical music. That's why it became so popular; audiences saw it as entertainment as well as art. Only two percent of Americans attend live opera—down from three percent twenty years ago. Nearly seventeen percent go to musical theater, the most popular of all the performing arts.

Does its small size spell doom for American opera? Not yet: two percent of the U.S. population represents over 5 million adults—not an inconsiderable audience. But the declining attendance trends reflect a change in the public's relationship to the art. Opera's audience remains large and passionate, but it is increasingly homebound. Attending opera is a difficult and expensive undertaking. Live opera happens mostly in large cities on a limited number of afternoons and evenings. The San Francisco Opera, the nation's second largest company, presents only fifty performances each year. Small companies may offer fewer than a dozen presentations in their full season. Most people experience opera through recordings, film, and broadcasts. Aficionados often listen to opera regularly without attending a performance for years.

Of all the traditional performing arts, opera is probably the one most deeply affected by technology. The art is remarkably malleable. Opera's power comes through on television and film with little loss in impact, though the viewing experience becomes solitary rather than communal. Spectacle is an important aspect of live performance, but audio recording has an astonishing ability to convey opera, often with a greater intimacy than one experiences in actual performance, especially in large venues. Technology allows listeners to move through time and space to hear the music. The first commercial recording of a full opera occurred in 1903 when HMV released Verdi's *Ernani*. (The earliest aria was recorded in 1889.) There are one hundred thirty years of opera performances available. There is also a continuous stream of new live opera broadcasts from around the world. The experience of opera now overwhelmingly occurs outside the opera house. Physical attendance has become the exception in what is now a metaphysical art.

Until the advent of recorded sound and broadcast, opera had always been a live social activity. One watched the performance as a member of a crowd in a public space. The audience and its reaction became part of the individual operagoer's experience. The later electronic audience, however, is invisible, atomized, and mostly solitary. One can measure the live audience. Most opera houses keep records of their annual attendance; most national arts councils, such as our National Endowment for the Arts, publish statistics on attendance and audience composition. At present, those statistics reveal how small and fragile the U.S. audience has become.

No one can reliably measure the invisible audience; they exist on their own multifarious terms. Electronic listeners are not bound by time or space. They might enjoy live broadcasts, but they are not limited to the repertory currently being produced. They can hear or see any work that has been recorded or filmed—whenever or wherever they want. I suspect they are lonelier than traditional operagoers but nonetheless satisfied by their immense freedom to pursue their private passions.

I know an attorney in Montana who has a huge opera collection, including every pirate recording of Leyla Gencer, a Turkish soprano. Gencer sang on stage from 1950 to 1985, but she never gained a commercial recording contract. Except for a single disk of arias produced in Italy, all that survives of her distinguished career are live recordings, made either by the opera house or by audience members on amateur equipment. When my friend listens to her performances of Donizetti's *Caterina Cornaro* or Bellini's *I Puritani*, he is probably the only person in the world doing so that evening. That fact does not diminish his pleasure or Gencer's artistry.

A small audience does not make an art less important, but small size can foster difficulties, not the least of which is that artists grow comfortable staying within their own coterie. (This tendency has damaged both contemporary opera and poetry.) Artists lose touch with the larger goals and human hungers that originally animated their art. They concentrate on displaying their command of current conventions. However constrained by its economic or social situation, an art form must remain ambitious in its sympathies and prodigal in imagination. Otherwise, it dissipates and decays. Opera began as the narrowest sort of coterie art—local, aristocratic, and ephemeral—but from the start, it sought to portray stories that explored the mysteries of existence. Often created for a single performance to a small audience, the earliest operas presented enduring myths of love, death, suffering, and transformation—Daphne, Orpheus, and Ulysses. Although opera became a larger and more elaborate medium, it never became deeper than its visionary origins.

CHAPTER XV

Still a Foreign Art

The composer who is frightened of losing his
audience through contact with a mass audience
is no longer aware of the meaning of art.

—AARON COPLAND

THE FIRST OPERA PERFORMED IN AMERICA WAS STAGED
in 1735 in Charleston, South Carolina—*Flora*, a ballad
opera imported from England. In 1757, the first opera
written by an American, William Smith's *Alfred*, premiered in Philadelphia. It was a pastiche with tunes
lifted from Handel, Arne, and others. Neither work has
any claim on posterity except its premiere date. The
most interesting thing about *Flora* and *Alfred* is that
they predate the American republic.

The early history of American opera consists
mostly of attempts to present the classics of European
opera. Much of the work was done by immigrant artists such as Lorenzo Da Ponte, usually with the same
results—a few exciting performances followed by bank-
ruptcy. Operas composed by Americans played little
role in this history. They were performed, and they
vanished. Nothing survives of the early works except
dates, titles, and unopened scores.

Opera has been popular in the United States for two hundred years. In the mid-nineteenth century it was not an elite art but a popular form of musical entertainment. Even as the audience shrank in the twentieth century, opera continued to inspire huge civic investment. Public and private money combined to build impressive opera houses and support the expensive musical organizations they require. No major American city could be seen as sophisticated without an art museum, symphony orchestra, and opera company—the gold stars of municipal maturity. Meanwhile conservatories and universities trained legions of singers, and a growing stream of new American works were commissioned and premiered to build a national repertory.

What has been the result? Opera remains a foreign art form in the United States. The works performed in American opera houses today are still mostly classics written by foreigners performed in foreign languages, often with the leading roles sung by foreigners. It is nothing as simple as colonization. Americans are singing and conducting in European and Asian opera houses where the audiences also hear works in foreign languages. Opera is an international art. America has been assimilated into the world system.

Seen from a global perspective, however, America is no operatic superpower. There are as many Czech operas in the international repertory as American ones. At the turn of the twenty-first century, only two American works were firmly established in the global repertory—Gershwin's *Porgy and Bess* and Menotti's *Amahl and the Night Visitors.* To that pair, one might have awarded provisional status to Philip Glass's "Portrait Trilogy," *Einstein on the Beach* (1976), *Satyagraha* (1979), and *Akhnaten* (1983). By 2000, those Minimalist spectacles had already carved a niche at major houses and international festivals.

Now that a quarter of the new century has passed, the situation has actually worsened. There will soon be only one American work in the global repertory. The Christian theme of Menotti's *Amahl* has reduced its appeal in today's secular opera houses. The Glass operas are still being produced, but the demanding requirements make them difficult for small houses to mount.

Each of these American export operas is unusual by traditional standards. Much of their appeal is how different they are from the European repertory. *Amahl and the Night Visitors* is a short family opera written for television as a Christmas special; it is swift, intimate, and accessible—an opera made for camera cuts and close-ups. Although Menotti's music is Italianate, his sentimental and hopeful libretto is as American as a sitcom. *Porgy and Bess* has spoken dialogue like a Broadway musical with a succession of individually framed songs. The work has melodies as sweeping as anything in Verdi or Puccini, but shaped by jazz, blues, and spirituals, the music doesn't sound like anything in the European repertory. *Porgy* is now always performed with a black cast, another factor which makes it distinctive in most international productions.

The Glass "Portraits" are not simply operas. They are long and elaborate musical spectacles done in collaboration with producer Robert Wilson. Their intricate visual elements (direction, design, and choreography) are essential parts of the operas. The music cannot be detached from the productions without fundamentally changing the nature of the works. In artistic terms, Wilson's contributions are equal to Glass's score. His production represents a visual libretto.

The short list of international favorites leads to another observation: it is significant that no American opera composed in the traditional European manner, such as Barber's *Vanessa* or Floyd's *Susannah*, has been incorporated into the global repertory. Why would Italy need *Susannah* when they have *verismo* masterpieces of their own? Why would Tokyo need *Vanessa* when it can produce *The Makropolous Affair* or *Fedora*?

Let's not blame the foreigners. Let's look at ourselves. American opera houses have not fostered a national repertory. There have never been so many new American operas appearing, but these commissions have little lasting impact. Companies enjoy the prestige and publicity of premieres, but they rarely champion older American works. The one large company that had consistently labored to build a national repertory, the New York City Opera, went bankrupt in 2013 after years of financial troubles. (It was revived a few years later as a smaller, community-based production group with minimal operations and fixed overhead.) The New York City Opera once devoted an entire season to American works. In 1958, supported by the Ford Foundation, the company produced ten American operas, only one of which was a world premiere. No other company has ever attempted anything as ambitious. The season was an artistic success and a financial failure. The house was often half-full or less. But the company's determination to give new operas a second production helped secure the future for a few American works such as *Susannah* and *The Ballad of Baby Doe*.

The Met announced a similar plan to support new opera in the 2023–24 season. It produced five contemporary operas, with no world premieres, as well as a staged version of John Adams's oratorio, *El Niño*. The company has announced another four recent works for the 2024–25 season, including the world premiere of Jeanine Tesori's *Grounded*. This new policy is a bold departure for a company that has often had no American works in its repertory. Will the new strategy have a lasting impact on the repertory? It certainly can't hurt. Will it increase ticket sales? New productions usually create a short-term bump in attendance, but they are more expensive to mount than old stagings. In the Met's case, economic considerations matter. The company has a huge and growing deficit. Like the earlier New York City Opera all-American season, the Met's sudden emphasis on new American works was driven by financial desperation. After the COVID quarantine, much of the Met's audience did not return. New works, it hopes, will attract new and younger people. The initial results, however, have been no more encouraging than the earlier NYCO experiment. For its 2023–2024 season, five of the six worst attended productions were new works.

Go to Vienna, St. Petersburg, or Madrid, and one finds rich national repertories of locally popular operas. These indigenous works may not be international favorites, but they occupy an important place in local affection and esteem. In Vienna, the *Staatsoper* presents the global repertory. Its season resembles those of Covent Garden, Paris Opera, or the Metropolitan. But the Austrian capital has a second major opera house, *Die Volksoper* or "People's Opera." This theater is dedicated mostly to composers of the Austro-Hungarian region, such as Johann Strauss, Franz Lehár, Robert Stolz, and Emmerich Kálmán. In Spanish-speaking countries, opera companies consider the *zarzuela* (in which song and spoken dialogue are mixed) as standard fare. The *zarzuelas* of Federico Chueca, Pablo Luna, and Amadeo Vives are rarely performed outside the Spanish-speaking world, but they remain popular from Mexico to Madrid. Russia has a large national repertory of works by composers of international stature, including Nikolai Rimsky-Korsakov, Mikhail Glinka, Modest Mussorgsky, Sergei Prokofiev, and Rodion Shchedrin. Rarely produced abroad, they account for half of most Russian operatic seasons.

Significantly, even the United Kingdom has developed a national operatic repertory—made up mostly of modern works. As in the case of Russia or Austria, it includes a few works with international presence, but mostly it consists of operas of domestic popularity. There are a few older classics, such as Henry Purcell's *Dido and Aeneas* (1689), and the Gilbert and Sullivan operettas, which have remained popular even after the demise of the D'Oyly Carte Opera Company in 1982. Most of the British repertory was composed after World War II. Benjamin Britten dominates the list with *Peter Grimes, The Turn of the Screw, Midsummer Night's Dream*, and *Noye's Fludde*, but there are also works by Michael Tippett, William Walton, Thomas Adès, Jonathan Dove, Judith Weir, George Benjamin, and others. The U.K. has only one-fifth the population of the United States, but London has usually offered more opera performances annually than New York, Berlin, or Paris (though the recent financial crisis at the English National Opera may jeopardize that leadership). There are other major companies in Glasgow, Cardiff, Leeds, and Birmingham as well as a national touring company. British operas always figure prominently in the seasons, often supported by BBC broadcasts and wide critical coverage. Perhaps the U.K.'s smaller size has been an advantage. Certainly the organizational genius of Britten helped. (His Aldeburgh Festival has continued strong since the composer's death in 1976; it produces contemporary British operas nearly every year.)

In the United States a few older operas hold a precarious position on the margins of repertory. According to a ten-year cumulative performance survey in 2016, the ten most often produced American operas were mostly familiar mid-century favorites—Menotti's

Amahl (1951), *The Consul* (1950), and *The Medium* (1946), Carlisle Floyd's *Susannah* (1955), George Gershwin's *Porgy and Bess* (1935), Douglas Moore's *The Ballad of Baby Doe* (1956), Samuel Barber's *Vanessa* (1958), Robert Ward's *The Crucible* (1961), Leonard Bernstein's *Candide* (1956–74), and Mark Adamo's *Little Women* (1998). I repeat the premiere dates to demonstrate how old these works are. Granted it was a cumulative survey that summarized a decade of performances, but it is significant that it contained no work premiered in the current century. The list also overstated the public presence of these American classics. Few productions happened in major houses (as do the national operas of Europe). Most of these operas survive in regional companies, college programs, and conservatories. Even in this small and supportive world, some of these standards are slipping away. Who wants to sit through *Baby Doe* without a star soprano?

CHAPTER XVI

Our Unheard Repertory

> Opera is built on one of the great
> natural equalities, namely the equality
> of men's and women's voices.
>
> —WILLA CATHER

MANY HISTORICALLY IMPORTANT AMERICAN OPERAS are rarely performed. Significant but neglected works include Scott Joplin's *Treemonisha* (1911), Deems Taylor's *The King's Henchman* (1927), Virgil Thomson's *Four Saints in Three Acts* (1928), Louis Gruenberg's *The Emperor Jones* (1933), Kurt Weill's *Street Scene* (1946), Marc Blitzstein's *Regina* (1949), William Grant Still's *Troubled Island* (1949), Aaron Copland's *The Tender Land* (1954), Hugo Weisgall's *Six Characters in Search of an Author* (1959), Jack Beeson's *Lizzie Borden* (1965), Samuel Barber's *Antony and Cleopatra* (1966), Lee Hoiby's *Summer and Smoke* (1971), and Alva Henderson's *Medea* (1972). One might augment this "legion of the lost ones" by nationalizing Australian-born Peggy Glanville-Hicks, who spent her most productive years in the U.S. and composed two splendid but neglected operas, *The Transposed Heads* (1953) and *Nausicaa* (1961).

Most new operas are premiered and never produced again. The real influence comes from companies that stage the rare second or third production of a new work. A few recent American operas have managed to secure an ongoing existence, most notably John Adams's *Nixon in China*, Philip Glass's *Akhnaten*, David Conte's *The Gift of the Magi*, and Anthony Davis's *X: The Life and Times of Malcolm X*. The most widely produced American opera of the new century is Jake Heggie's *Dead Man Walking*. Premiered in San Francisco in 2000, it has had over seventy productions. In 2023, the Met opened its season with it, a distinction given previously to only three other American operas in its one hundred forty-four-year history—*Peter Ibbetson, Antony and Cleopatra*, and *The Fire Shut Up in My Bones*. Whether Heggie's opera can sustain a position in the repertory remains unknown. Its predecessors at the Met's opening night do not fill one with optimism.

In all these measures of operatic popularity, one can't help noting the absence of women composers. There is no opera by a woman in the core repertory. Nor does a woman composer appear among the up-and-coming favorites. Where are Peggy Glanville-Hicks, Thea Musgrave, Lori Laitman, Rene Orth, Jennifer Higdon, Meredith Monk, Libby Larsen, and Jeanine Tesori? Is there not any opera by an American woman worth regular revival? For whatever reasons, innocent or nefarious, music critics have been reluctant to champion operas by women composers. It has been a long-standing bias. After the triumphant premiere of

Glanville-Hicks's *Nausicaa* at the 1961 Athens Festival, the opera received enormous coverage, overwhelmingly positive, across the international press and broadcast media. Despite all the praise, the composer noted:

> Almost all of these men (critics) have the word "masterpiece" on the tip of their tongues, and simply can't bring themselves to come out with it as applying to a woman composer. It sticks in their gullets.

No artist is an objective judge of his or her own reviews, but there is something more than self-regard in Glanville-Hicks's complaint. Like many other female composers, especially in the mid-twentieth century, she was assigned to a marginal category, not quite equal to the big boys. Sixty years later, the situation is not simply a cultural scandal; it is a kind of paradox. Why is the American opera world fifty years behind the social trends of poetry, dance, and theater?

The most widely performed American operas remain traditional in both musical and dramatic terms. For decades, the musical intelligentsia bemoaned that American opera eschewed progressive compositional trends. As Eric Salzman complained in *Twentieth Century Music* (1974), "Opera, long at the leading edge of musical development, has become an ultra-conservative institution, resistant to change and highly dependent on routine." (Drama critics would have said something equally harsh had they paid any attention to American opera libretti.) As performance statistics demonstrate, the situation has changed little in the half century since Salzman's lament. The tonal and melodic operas of Menotti, Floyd, Barber, Bernstein, and Moore remain popular; and the newer works that followed them into the repertory (by composers such as Adamo, Conte, Heggie, and Laitman) are also traditional in style. Even the leading Minimalists, such as Glass, Adams, and David Lang, who disrupted the operatic establishment in the 1980s, were resolutely tonal, though their compositional procedures were novel. Part of Minimalism's innovation was literary. It rejected the Naturalism that typified the libretti of most American operas whether by conservative or progressive composers. It created highly stylized forms of theater more influenced by ritual than realism.

American opera still exists in a parallel tradition, more populist and conservative than symphonic music, though the stylistic gap has narrowed in the past thirty years. In the opera world, academic Modernism went down in total defeat. American serialism, the twelve-tone compositional technique developed by Arnold Schoenberg, has vanished without leaving a single opera in the national canon. By the late 1980s, Minimalism became the new avant-garde trend in opera. Unlike serialism, it achieved its notable innovations in accessible styles. In the mythology of Modernism, obtuse audiences reject new artistic developments. The success of Minimalism was a reminder how often classical audiences welcome new styles of music.

American opera has been confined by the institutions that support it. The major opera houses were built primarily to present and preserve the established classics of Europe. Neither they nor their repertory grew organically from American culture. The size and stature of our major companies, even perhaps their high standards of excellence, make them unreliable incubators for artistic innovation. The Metropolitan Opera, for example, is a magnificent institution, but it has a terrible record for commissioning new works. Of the three dozen operas premiered by the Met, only one American work has survived, just barely, at the low end of the repertory—Barber's *Vanessa*.

Perhaps the Metropolitan Opera's poor record is not a coincidence but a function of its size and complexity. The qualities necessary to move a new project through the Met's complicated system are not the same virtues that will make a work, especially an innovative one, succeed. Not the least of these things are the literary elements. A librettist has less influence than a lighting director in terms of a new production. The projects originate less from artists than from management. The inclinations of the opera company, however, may not be the needs of the composer. Not all new operas require a 110-piece orchestra, full choir, or vast stage. In its abundant resources, the Met has a tendency to infect most new ideas with gigantism. They want to use the army of artistic personnel they so expensively maintain.

There is at present a great wave of new opera in America. Faced with aging and declining audiences, a long-term trend accelerated by the pandemic quarantine, opera companies feel an urgency to reassert their relevance. They hope to attract younger audiences with contemporary works that address current topics and ideas. They also understand the potential power of presenting operas in English. Significantly, the current creative strategy relies more on the libretto than the music. Companies want new operas that embody new perspectives. In theory, the trend should be good news for writers. It isn't. For these theme-driven projects, literary quality matters less than the fashionable subject matter and theatrical concepts. It is not uncommon for a new libretto to consist of a collage of texts assembled by the director, as in Peter Sellar's selection from declassified government documents, poems, Sanskrit classics, and Tewa native song for John Adams's *Doctor Atomic*. It seems unlikely that new operas that privilege the directorial concept over the music and poetry will have longevity.

It is impossible to predict how long the recent enthusiasm for new works will last. Perhaps it signals a permanent change in operatic programming. Nearly all of the standard repertory is more than a hundred years old. In a living art form, the canon should be constantly renewed. Until the early twentieth century, the operatic repertory was in a continual state of innovation and expansion. The public followed new composers and operas with passionate attention. A young talent, such as Mascagni, Korngold, or Weill could gain international celebrity with a single work. American opera may indeed be reinventing itself, though it's hard to believe that meaningful transformation will come from the bureaucracies that run the Met and other major companies. Their historical record is unimpressive. The last major operatic movement, Minimalism, developed mostly outside institutional and academic culture. The operas of Glass, Lang, and Meredith Monk emerged in bohemian downtown New York, a milieu which is itself fading into the past.

Such is the situation of the American composer or librettist. Opera is nearly invisible in the United States, especially new opera. It appeals to a tiny and declining audience, augmented by a somewhat larger group who experience opera through film or recording. The repertory of American opera houses consists mostly of older, European operas. There is an acknowledged need for renewal, but no proven strategy has emerged. The theatrical and ideological aspects of new opera have become as important as the music and libretto. The literary elements, especially when they involve poetry, face critical indifference or condescension. The country now has over two hundred companies, but it still hasn't developed a national repertory. The only thing secure in the future of American opera is the deficit.

CHAPTER XVII

American Opera Begins

America has never quite trusted opera.
It was brought over from Europe, after all,
by Americans who had the gall to find
homegrown entertainments inadequate.

—MATTHEW AUCOIN

AMERICAN OPERA BEGAN AS IMITATION OF EUROPEAN works, and so it remained until well into the twentieth century. The most interesting opera created in the first two decades of the last century wasn't produced at the Met. It wasn't produced anywhere. Scott Joplin wrote his opera, *Treemonisha*, in 1910 and published the piano-vocal score a year later at his own expense. In 1915, with no production in sight, he financed a concert reading of the score in Harlem with himself at the piano. The under-rehearsed performance proved a disaster. Joplin died two years later. The opera went unproduced until 1972.

Although *Treemonisha* won a posthumous Pulitzer Prize after its belated premiere, the opera is no masterpiece. The composer's libretto is clumsy, the dramatic structure ill proportioned. Joplin's theme is uplifting—

the importance of education for the newly liberated slaves in the rural South—but the plot lacks the emotional elements that animate musical theater. Nonetheless *Treemonisha* was a significant work. Its eclectic score prefigured the central ambition of later American opera—to create a new national style distinct from European models that mixed classical and popular sounds, especially from African American traditions. This goal was slow and intermittent in its realization, at least in part because African American composers had little representation in the operatic world. No black composer would be performed at the Met until the 2021 premiere of Terence Blanchard's *Fire Shut Up in My Bones*—106 years after Joplin's ill-fated Harlem concert.

The first capable champion of American opera was an Italian. When Giulio Gatti-Casazza, former director of La Scala, arrived in 1908 to lead the Metropolitan Opera, he inaugurated a campaign to promote American opera, which no native impresario would have considered. As an Italian, he understood that running a major opera house included presenting new works. He felt the United States was ready for a musical role on equal terms to Europe. A quiet man, who never learned much English, Gatti-Casazza was a formidable theatrical manager. He assembled a stellar company of singers, which included Enrico Caruso, Amelita Galli-Curci, Feodor Chaliapin, Tita Ruffo, and Rosa Ponselle; Arturo Toscanini and Gustav Mahler conducted the early seasons. (Even the Met wasn't big enough for two such colossal egos: Mahler soon left.) Gatti-Casazza staged world premieres by celebrated composers, including Puccini's *La Fanciulla del West* (1910), which had an American setting, and *Il Trittico* (1918). He also introduced Giordano's *Madame Sans-Gêne* (1915) and Engelbert Humperdinck's *Königskinder* (1910). These international premieres demonstrated America's new place in world opera as well as its ability to outbid the European competition for great composers and singers.

More ambitiously, Gatti-Casazza presented a series of new works by American composers in well-staged productions with the finest casts the Met could offer. He began by sponsoring a $10,000 prize for a new opera. It was a substantial award—worth over $300,000 today. Horatio Parker won with *Mona* (1912). Subsequent premieres included Walter Damrosch's *Cyrano* (1913), Reginald De Koven's *The Canterbury Pilgrims* (1917), Joseph Carl Breil's *The Legend* (1919), and Henry Kimball Hadley's *Cleopatra's Night* (1920). No one alive has seen a production of any of those pieces, all of which vanished after their first season. It is slow and uncertain work to create a national tradition.

Gatti-Casazza's later productions had greater public impact, though like their predecessors, none survives in the repertory. In 1933 he gave Howard Hanson's *Merry Mount* its staged premiere after the opera's success in a concert performance in Ann Arbor. *Merry Mount* earned more curtain calls—fifty in total—than any opera in the Met's history but the work never gained another professional production. The opera was too long and dark for most audiences, and the score was stronger for its choral passages than in the solo writing. Hanson preserved the musical themes in a popular orchestral suite, but, like most American operas, it soon became impossible to hear the opera itself. Until conductor Gerard Schwarz recorded *Merry Mount* in 2007, the opera was preserved only in an incomplete 1934 radio broadcast in the Met archives. There is a sad irony that the Met tape was made available only after Schwarz's recording appeared.

Deems Taylor's two operas, *The King's Henchman* (1927) and *Peter Ibbetson* (1931), played to sold-out houses and went on tour. *The King's Henchman* is remembered now because its best-selling libretto was written by Edna St. Vincent Millay, the first woman author to be produced at the Met. (The Harper & Brothers edition sold through four printings in the first twenty days.) There has been no commercial recording of *The King's Henchman*, except a pair of short scenes performed by baritone Lawrence Tibbett on two sides of a single 78 disk. (There is also an almost unlistenable pirate recording of highlights—mostly snaps, crackles, and pops— dubbed by a listener from a 1942 radio broadcast.) *Peter Ibbetson* survives in a clear but scratchy 1934 broadcast recording with its distinguished first cast (which included Tibbett, Lucrezia Bori, and Edward Johnson). None of these recordings, except the Tibbett 78 single, was commercially released. I mention the details of the recordings to demonstrate the poor documentation of early American opera.

Gatti-Casazza's twenty-seven-year tenure at the Met ended in 1935. His retirement ended the Met's commitment to American opera. Under his leadership, the company had presented fifteen American works, including thirteen world premieres. In the half-century after his departure, the Met introduced only four new American works. The Met sank into what Joseph Horowitz has called "the culture of performance." The company pursued virtuoso singing and strong orchestral support rather than musical creativity. Nonetheless, Gatti-Casazza's long campaign helped foster a burst of operatic innovation in the 1930s. The first distinctively American operas emerged—works that would not have been created elsewhere.

The best new operas of the decade appeared suddenly within a three-year span—Louis Gruenberg's *The Emperor Jones* (1933), Virgil Thomson's *Four Saints in Three Acts* (1934), and George Gershwin's *Porgy and Bess* (1935). The three works form an odd group. The operas show no common musical tendency; they are strikingly different in style; they range from atonality to the simplest sort of tonality. Their libretti, however, share powerful similarities. First, all three works employ exceptionally strong literary texts by Eugene O'Neill, Gertrude Stein, and the team of DuBose Heyward and Ira Gershwin. Each libretto holds its own with the music. Second, all three operas draw on the power of African American culture. Their affinities with Black culture, however, appear more in their literary and theatrical elements—plot, characters, setting, and casting—than in their music. Only Gershwin uses blues, jazz, and spirituals as foundational elements in his score (which also draws from the Broadway tradition). African American music has only intermittent presence in Gruenberg and Thomson; their operas present African American elements mostly in visual and dramatic terms. In all three works, however, the use of African American casts on an operatic stage in that era represented a huge cultural and political breakthrough. Finally, the operas share another common element: each creative team included one or more Jewish artists. Until then, the creation of American opera had been mostly a WASP affair.

The first of these breakthrough works was Gruenberg's *The Emperor Jones*, Gatti-Casazza's last and boldest American premiere. Gruenberg and Kathleen de Jaffa (who translated libretti for the Met) "adapted" Eugene O'Neill's expressionistic one-act play for musical setting. In fact, they simply edited the playwright's text; nearly all of the language is O'Neill's. *The Emperor Jones* presents the savage story of Brutus Jones, a black American convict who escapes to a Caribbean island where he sets himself up as a dictator. Produced in 1920 by the Provincetown Players with a black cast, *The Emperor Jones* was O'Neill's first box office success. The title role soon became associated with Paul Robeson who starred in New York and London revivals. His film version appeared in the same year as the opera.

Gruenberg admired Arnold Schoenberg. In 1923 he had conducted the American premiere of *Pierrot*

Lunaire, which had required twenty-two rehearsals. His operatic score was unabashedly Modernist—violent, dissonant, and often atonal, though at one point it interpolates a Negro spiritual, "It's Me, O Lord, Standin' in de Need of Prayer." The Met had never heard anything like *The Emperor Jones*. (Alban Berg's *Wozzeck* would not be performed there until 1959; Schoenberg's *Erwartung* waited until 1989.) Propulsive, bold, and dramatic, *The Emperor Jones* was an immediate success with the Met audience. Gruenberg's stark score amplified the already considerable power of O'Neill's play. The Met's star baritone Lawrence Tibbett, now famous in Hollywood as well as opera, played the title role in blackface. At Tibbett's insistence, dancers from the New Negro Art Theater were featured rather than the Met's all-white regulars. *The Emperor Jones* was broadcast, revived the next year, and then taken on the Met tour. The opera had numerous productions both in America and abroad. Tibbett's recording of the spiritual became modern American opera's first hit single. Reviewing the premiere, Olin Downes perfectly summarized Gruenberg's achievement: "The music is prodigiously sure, headlong, fantastical, brutal in its approach; yet masterly in contrast of mood and in its main proportions." Now neglected, *Emperor Jones* has the distinction of being the first significant Modernist American opera. The only full recording is in Italian from a 1951 production in Rome—a particularly bizarre demonstration of how little America values its operatic heritage.

Gruenberg's later career testifies to the limited

opportunities open to American opera composers of his generation. After the success of *The Emperor Jones*, he wrote *Green Mansions* (1937), a radio opera for CBS. Radio (and later television) seemed attractive venues to composers of the period. Each of the major networks maintained a symphony orchestra, choirs, and singers. All programmed classical music. The trouble was that a single broadcast was insufficient to support a new opera unless the work also received theatrical productions. *Green Mansions* was never heard after its radio premiere.

In 1937, Gruenberg moved to Los Angeles, which had become a haven for émigré composers such as Schoenberg, Stravinsky, Rachmaninov, and Korngold. He began writing music for Hollywood films in addition to his classical works. Gruenberg scored eleven films, including *Arch of Triumph* (1948) and *All the King's Men* (1949). He received three Academy Award nominations. His scores were also recycled, without credit, as stock music for numerous B-films, such as *Valley of the Head Hunters* (1953) and *Devil Goddess* (1955). He continued to compose serious music, including a jazz-inflected romantic violin concerto (1945) for Jascha Heifetz, a fellow Angeleno. Gruenberg remained dedicated to opera. He wrote six later operas, including *Volpone* and *Anthony and Cleopatra*. None were ever produced. He died at eighty in Beverly Hills in 1964.

Thirteen months after *The Emperor Jones*, Virgil Thomson's *Four Saints in Three Acts* premiered in Hartford. The opera's unlikely venue was the work of Arthur

Everett "Chick" Austin Jr., the curator of the Hartford Atheneum, America's first art museum. In 1928 Austin launched an organization called "The Friends and Enemies of Modern Music," to sponsor concerts of works by living composers in a town not known for its progressive taste. (Local insurance executive Wallace Stevens became a member.) Austin hoped to create a Ballets Russes style dance company with George Balanchine, who had just arrived from Europe. The project never succeeded, but Austin nonetheless brought leading edge art and music to the sleepy office town.

Four Saints in Three Acts was Austin's first major theatrical production. Against all the odds, he produced, with limited funds and little staff, a radically original opera that attracted international notice. Perhaps this feat came about through Austin's training as a professional magician—but mostly it resulted from qualities he possessed that large organizations lack: superb individual taste, an eye for innovative talent, and an appetite for risk. In Hartford, he had already organized the first American retrospective of Picasso. Later in Sarasota, Florida, when Austin led the new Ringling Museum of Art, he inexpensively acquired masterpieces of Baroque painting, a period which major American museums then ignored.

If Gruenberg's adaptation of Eugene O'Neill was American opera's first successful Modernist work, Thomson's setting of Stein's lyric and elliptical text was our first avant-garde classic. The music of *Four Saints in Three Acts* is striking in its simplicity—four square and diatonic. Thomson's style is rooted in Protestant hymns, Catholic chant, and vaudeville; the African American elements in the score are minimal. The opera's innovation lay in its combination of populist music and experimental text with bold staging and casting. Stein's libretto is a masterpiece of wordplay and free association. With zany disregard for consistency, the opera features about twenty saints in four acts plus a prelude. The main characters are three sixteenth-century Spanish Catholic saints—Ignatius of Loyola and two Teresas of Avila—who are accompanied by several fictive saints, including Settlement, Chavez, and Plan. The original cast was all black, strongly supported by Eva Jessye's Harlem choir. The budget was tight, so the sets were made from cellophane, which shook and shimmered like a heavenly vision. There was no plot, only a set of fanciful situations expressed by song and dances. (Frederick Ashton did the choreography when Balanchine declined.) In a particularly charming touch, two godparents—Compère and Commère—sang the stage directions—another example of the text guiding the music. Well produced, *Four Saints in Three Acts* is irresistible in its queer celestial merriment.

A year later, Gershwin's *Porgy and Bess* previewed in Boston and soon moved to Broadway. The work was a critical success, financial disappointment, and immediate classic of American musical theater. The opera's achievement is too well known to require much commentary, but it helps to repeat a few obvious observations. Gershwin did something new and significant; he crafted an American operatic idiom that merged European, Jewish American (i.e., Tin Pan Alley), and African American musical styles. In collaboration with his librettists, he also brought the poetic power of popular song into opera in a way that animates the entire work. *Porgy and Bess* created the sound that American opera had been waiting to sing.

Most reviewers praised the show. Whatever their reservations, they understood the breakthrough Gershwin's opera represented. Virgil Thomson, however, gave the work a condescending assessment, tinged with racism, probably motivated by professional jealousy of Gershwin's many successes. Thomson objected to precisely those elements that made *Porgy and Bess* most original and influential:

> At best it is a piquant but highly unsavory stirring-up together of Israel, Africa and the Gaelic Isles . . . I do not like fake folklore, nor bittersweet harmony, nor six-part choruses, nor fidgety accompaniments, nor gefilte-fish orchestration.

Porgy and Bess is not a perfect work, but in its best moments—in "Summertime," for example, or "Bess, You Is My Woman"—the music is sublime. As the philosopher Longinus observed in his first century treatise, *On the Sublime*, when great art takes your soul into the joyful exaltation, small imperfections do not matter. The ecstatic emotions, he observed, bring the audience beyond rationality. Under such circumstances, only a pedant (or rival composer) cares if some passages go awry. Gershwin's "unsavory stirring" of Africa and "gefilte-fish orchestration" proved popular. Despite its imperfections, *Porgy and Bess* has become the most popular American opera in the world.

There was a fourth premiere in the thirties that promised another important work—Marc Blitzstein's *The Cradle Will Rock* (1937). Commissioned by the WPA Theatre Group, the musical play aspired to be a proletarian operetta. He aimed in particular to create an American equivalent of Brecht and Weill's *The Threepenny Opera*, which combined cabaret, popular song, traditional opera, and political satire. (Blitzstein would brilliantly translate that work into an English-language performing version.) If Blitzstein had achieved his goal, he would have created a new genre of American opera, an operetta so self-knowing and ironic about its own procedures that it would have transcended its populist genre. It would be seen as high art, as Brecht and Weill so deftly managed in their eclectic collaborations.

No American opera ever had a more exciting premiere—perhaps no opera ever. Directed by Orson Welles and produced by John Houseman, the work gained enormous publicity, especially among the American Left, during a series of benefit previews. On the day of the premiere Blitzstein found his venue, Maxine Elliott's Theatre, locked by the WPA, which feared a political backlash. Guards had been posted to prevent Houseman from removing the costumes and props, which were declared federal property. Welles and Houseman led the opening night patrons on a twenty-block hike to the Venice Theatre. The crowd grew as Welles invited passersby to attend the performance for free. At the theater the musicians' union orchestra members then refused to play unless Houseman could guarantee their full salary. Meanwhile the actors and singers were told by their union, Actor's Equity, not to appear on stage unless the production was re-sanctioned by the WPA. Blitzstein outwitted the federal censorship by performing the work on a piano while cast members in their street clothes sang their parts from seats in the theater.

Most of the audience couldn't follow the weirdly disembodied performance beyond its pro-labor and anti-capitalist politics, but the real-world drama of the premiere made them ecstatic. It was agit-prop's finest hour. The press coverage was massive. Blitzstein had everything he needed for a classic except credible words and music. His libretto was heavy-handed, even for Marxist propaganda. There was no attempt to individualize the characters (Mr. Mister, Reverend Salvation, Editor Daily, President Prexy, etc.). They remained cartoon figures with no tangible humanity on stage. The songs were perfunctory, especially compared to the incisive lyrics and sardonic music of *The Threepenny Opera*. (Simultaneously funny, savage, tender, and revelatory, the Brecht-Weill work is a masterpiece of irony—a quality nearly absent in Blitzstein's piece.) The work's legendary status has inspired revivals at ten-year intervals. Theater afficionados are curious; they want to like it. I know I did. Even with strong casts and special pleading, *The Cradle Will Rock* is a dud.

Gershwin's death at thirty-nine, two years after the premiere of *Porgy and Bess*, not only robbed the world of his unwritten music; it dimmed a promising possibility in American opera—the creation of a style that would combine European opera, Broadway musical, and African American music into a new national idiom different from anything in the Old World. Gershwin prompted a recognition that opera could be renewed by the energy of popular music. Some composers tried to follow him in works as dissimilar as *The Cradle Will Rock*, Weill's *Street Scene*, and William Grant Still's *Troubled Island*. Finding the right formula proved difficult.

CHAPTER XVIII

Can Opera Talk?

*I write musical theater. The trouble with saying
Broadway is that it has a pejorative context.*

—STEPHEN SONDHEIM

THERE IS A BASIC QUESTION ABOUT GERSHWIN'S *PORGY
and Bess* that has haunted American musical theater.
What is *Porgy*? Is it an opera, operetta, or musical?
Most productions and editions of the work avoid an
answer. They simply state, "Music by George Gershwin,
Libretto by DuBose Heyward, Lyrics by DuBose Heyward and Ira Gershwin." There is an obvious reluctance
to place the work in a specific category. (The publisher
knows that musicals make more money than operas.)
In a few instances, however, the work is called "a folk
opera," which was Gershwin's own description.

The term "folk opera" refers to the European genre
of sung theater that borrows musical material of a
specific region or people—melodies, modal scales, or
dance rhythms—to create operas of popular appeal
that reflect national identity. Bedřich Smetana's *The
Bartered Bride* (1866), for example, used Czech dance
rhythms and melodic patterns that his regional audi-

ence recognized as their own. Gustav Holst's opera, *The Wandering Scholar* (1934), likewise based its style on English folk music, though it never quotes any actual folk tunes. Gershwin used the term both to claim operatic status for *Porgy and Bess* and to acknowledge the work's debt to African American music. A musicologist might debate how accurate the term "folk opera" is in this case. The pointed Gershwin/Heyward lyrics have a Tin Pan Alley polish that hardly feels folkloric. But it helps to know where the composer stood. The question matters because *Porgy* has inspired many subsequent works of American musical theater whose popular sources have complicated their identity.

The problem is older than *Porgy*. When Joplin published the score of *Treemonisha*, he subtitled it an "Opera in Three Acts," although the work resembled operetta far more than traditional opera. Joplin understood that opera had greater prestige. The genre of a musical work establishes specific expectations for the audience, performers, and critics. Joplin wanted *Treemonisha* regarded as a serious work of art, not as a musical entertainment.

The concept of genre is important because it suggests what formal elements a composer and librettist might bring to new works. In American opera that question becomes complicated when creators want to incorporate elements from popular music and theater. It confuses the frame of reference. *Porgy* has spoken dialogue; it also has self-contained songs. Both of those features associate it with the Broadway musical.

Traditional opera generally sets the entire libretto to music. How far can a composer depart from the conventional model of opera before the audience changes its perspective on the work? Must every word be sung for the work to be serious?

Critics tend to deny any work with substantial dialogue the title of opera. Real operas should have continuous music to guide the drama without relying on dialogue to move the plot. Depending on the context, a piece with spoken dialogue is labeled an operetta, musical, *Singspiel*, or *zarzuela*—all less exalted categories than opera. The criteria seem clear, but, in practice, they are applied inconsistently. Many classic musical works escape the downgrade.

No one refers to *The Magic Flute* as a *Singspiel*, even though it has a great deal of dialogue. Three factors elevate *The Magic Flute* to the status of opera. First, the score shows Mozart in the full maturity of his genius. Second, in addition to its low comedy, the work has a Masonic subplot with music of undeniable nobility. Third, *The Magic Flute* was Mozart's last opera, and no one wants the *divino maestro* to have checked out writing an operetta. Likewise, Carl Orff's *Die Kluge* (*The Clever Girl*) and *Der Mond* (*The Moon*), both of which have dialogue, earned the honorific by the brilliance of their music and the parable-like quality of their libretti. Based on two folk tales from the Brothers Grimm, the operas have a tough edge and dark vision that no one would associate with operetta or children's theater.

There is a theoretical bias among critics that opera

should be entirely sung. It keeps things simple: opera is sung, theater is spoken, popular musical theater mixes the two modes. The problem is that the history of the standard repertory doesn't reflect this neat division. The problem isn't just with Mozart. Many famous operas have dialogue; many more once had spoken elements that were removed or altered by producers, often without the composer's consent. Beethoven's *Fidelio*, Donizetti's *La Fille du Régiment*, Léo Delibes's *Lakmé*, Carl Maria von Weber's *Der Freischütz*, and Manuel de Falla's *La Vida Breve* all have dialogue. So, too, does Georges Bizet's *Carmen*, some of the time.

Carmen is always listed as an opera, and it is mostly performed with sung recitatives, but Bizet did not write it that way. When *Carmen* was first produced in 1875 at the Opéra-Comique in Paris, the work had spoken dialogue. Three months later the composer died at thirty-seven from heart failure. That same year his friend Ernest Guiraud replaced the dialogue with his own recitatives for production in Vienna. That revision became the standard international version. Meanwhile, the original version continued to be performed in France at the Opéra-Comique and in the provinces. *Carmen's* lurid plot and tragic ending set it apart from standard operettas, but Guiraud's posthumous additions certified its status as a real opera. The new score did not reflect Bizet's creative vision, only the house style in Vienna. In recent years, the original version of *Carmen* has often been revived. It delivers a different effect—tougher and more urgent than the Guiraud edition.

Few operas are performed exactly as the composer intended. They are cut for length, transposed for individual singers, reorchestrated by conductors, and censored by governments. (Then the directors get to work with their unpredictable improvements.) When the Paris Opera produced a work, the composer was obliged to set all dialogue to music and provide a ballet after the intermission. The changes rarely improved the original.

Charles Gounod's *Faust* (1859) was composed with dialogue between the musical numbers. A year later Gounod composed recitatives for German productions. The work was also retitled *Margarethe* or *Gretchen*, to avoid confusion with Ludwig Spohr's German-language version. Then, in 1869, the Paris Opera produced it with recitatives and a ballet. In this version, *Faust* became the most popular opera of the century. The ballet, expensive to produce and distracting to the dramatic structure, was gradually dropped in most productions. Consequently, a third version, never approved by the composer, is the standard score.

Modern critics have long been suspicious of the so-called "number opera," which unfolds as a series of individual songs and ensembles—the standard form of popular musical theater from Broadway to the Danube. This aversion will puzzle the average operagoer. Handel, Mozart, Rossini, and other classic composers all wrote operas with distinct arias, duets, and ensembles. Indeed, arias constitute the most popular parts of opera. Many people listen to them who never enter an opera house. Most of opera's cultural presence comes from these excerpts. Like poetry, opera is mysteriously quotable. The high points of both arts can often survive removal from their original context. A few lines from a great poem evoke the power of the whole, an aria conveys much of the opera's lyric magic. Millions of people listen to the radiant high points of operas they will never see in performance. Are they missing something? Yes, but one should not underestimate the joy they receive. The human purposes of opera are not restricted to watching complete performances in a theater. The enchantments of song are so transportable that one wonders how the number opera fell into such ill repute.

The notion that serious opera required continuous music began in the late Romantic period with Richard Wagner. He developed a new style of opera to realize his vision of completely unified musical drama. Wagnerian opera never lets the audience go. The orchestra leads it forward, without interruption, through shifting, chromatic harmonies and endlessly unfolding melodic lines, all further unified by recurring thematic motifs. The effect is powerful, almost hypnotic. For many of the earliest listeners, the impact was Dionysian.

Wagner's compositional innovations were only part of his revisionist view of opera. He designed his own theater at Bayreuth. He eliminated the boxes, which had traditionally characterized the interior architecture of opera houses. Bayreuth had only one box—

for King Ludwig who had financed the construction. Instead, there were two thousand hard seats without armrests, all set in straight lines of sight to the stage. The huge orchestra was hidden. The lights were turned out just before the piece started. Until then, opera had been performed in lighted theaters where the audience members could observe each other. At Bayreuth, all attention focused on the stage. It was not an opera house; it was a temple of art. Like Yahweh, Wagner was a jealous god who allowed no strange gods before him. Only his operas were performed in his austere Festival Theatre. The opening of Bayreuth marked a historic shift in European drama. Opera was no longer entertainment. It was a sacred art.

The new Germanic style met initial resistance in Italy, still the epicenter of opera. Wagner's innovations intensified the historic debate between German fascination with symphonic elements and Italian emphasis on the human voice. His theatrical reforms also violated the social nature of Italian opera houses where opera was a communal as well as artistic occasion. Box owners often attended every performance in the season; their enjoyment of the music was inextricably mixed with seeing their friends and neighbors. Ultimately, Wagner's elevation of the composer and the art proved too seductive for late Romantics to resist. Opera had evolved into the most glamorous and extravagant art form in Europe. Composers had long felt trapped in the conventions imposed by impresarios, official censors, and audiences. When Italy's national composer, Giuseppe Verdi, adopted many of Wagner's techniques in his late operas, *Otello* (1887) and *Falstaff* (1893), Europe surrendered to the Old Sorcerer of Bayreuth. It had taken three centuries, but Germany had finally conquered Italy on the battlefield of opera.

Once the world's two operatic titans agreed on the procedure, the *durchkomponiert* or "through-composed" score became codified as the mandatory design for serious opera. The orchestra was expected to provide an ongoing foundation for the drama, unbroken by dialogue or separate vocal numbers. There was a critical and creative consensus that continuous scores were modern and progressive—the logical development of German musical genius. By contrast, the traditional Italian structure with arias and ensembles was retrograde and patronizing. The new consensus survived the transition from Romanticism into Modernism. It provided the structure for influential key works such as Debussy's *Pélleas et Mélisande* (1902), Béla Bartók's *Bluebeard's Castle* (1918), and Alban Berg's *Wozzeck* (1925). Indeed, the style still exercises a near monopoly on new opera in the twenty-first century.

When a modern opera contains a definable aria, such as *"Ch'ella mi creda"* in Puccini's masterfully through-composed *La Fanciulla del West* (1910) or *"Es gibt ein Reich"* in Strauss's *Ariadne auf Naxos* (1912), it emerges from and then returns to the underlying orchestra-driven design, interrupted only by applause. This was the method of the early twentieth-century composers such as Puccini, Strauss, and Janáček.

Strauss spoke for most of his contemporaries when he asserted that the aria was still "the soul of opera," but now it needed to be part of a seamless musical structure.

There were still a few significant modern works that presented self-contained songs, introduced by spoken dialogue, such as *Porgy and Bess, The Threepenny Opera, The Moon,* and *Street Scene.* Their style makes musicologists nervous; it recalls Broadway or even Viennese operetta, the favorite genres of the supposedly philistine middle classes. To what category does one assign such works? Each of these operas had to develop a strategy to avoid being demoted to mere entertainment. It was often a literary strategy that used plot, characterization, and verse style as much as musical innovation.

In *The Threepenny Opera,* Brecht and Weill escape the charge of commercial pandering by presenting criminals, prostitutes, and other deplorables who mocked middle-class values and pieties. Brecht's mordant lyrics were shocking, aggressive, and brilliant. Weill's music delighted—not always ironically—in the malevolence of the characters. Take, for example, the famous "Pirate Jenny" song, in which a maid at a filthy harbor hotel imagines herself a pirate queen. Jenny savors the murderous vengeance she will exact when her pirate crew levels the town and decapitates every inhabitant. *Porgy* demonstrated its artistic integrity by bringing the African American voice and experience to the segregated operatic stage. Orff's *The Moon* was a dark and macabre parable about death. Weill's *Street Scene* declared its serious identity by presenting the lives of poor and immigrant families given voice by Langston Hughes's lyrics. None of these strategies would have worked, of course, had not each opera had a strong and distinctive score.

The questions about spoken dialogue and self-contained songs are not academic. They influence artistic decisions. The through-composed opera and the number opera draw from different traditions—not just musically but also in literary terms. Each aesthetic is so different that the peak lyric moments in one style hardly resemble the other. In the symphonic tradition, the orchestra and voices rise in passionate climax, but the words, less important than the physical sound of the combined musical forces, are often lost. There is a joke about Strauss's *Elektra* that exists in several versions, each purporting to quote a different conductor or the composer himself: at the end of the performance, the maestro exclaims with satisfaction, "The orchestra played well tonight—you couldn't hear the singers." *Elektra* can probably survive such a performance, though few would consider it ideal. The orchestra and vocal lines convey the peak moments of anger and suffering, even if the words are muffled. (Strauss's use of operatic pantomime and image suffices to convey the dramatic situation.) No one conducting *The Threepenny Opera* would make the Strauss joke. Brecht's lyrics need to land for the audience to experience the work. In the number opera, the poetic impact of the lyrics matters.

Neither operatic style is inherently better than the other. Both are legitimate aesthetics with long legacies of masterpieces. Since the late nineteenth century, however, the through-composed technique has been considered superior. It is assumed to embody a more modern approach—the pure and bold aspirations of high art. By contrast, the number opera has been regarded as a backward form trapped in the mercenary instincts of popular entertainment. Does this once useful dichotomy still seem valid? Does the Wagnerian tradition still feel modern or progressive? Hasn't it become just another period style? Does contemporary opera need a full symphony playing continuously from start to finish?

The requirements of nineteenth-century grand opera are still reflected in the institutions that sustain opera. They employ huge orchestras and choirs, bigger than anything Mozart or Donizetti would have known. Opera houses have also grown bigger over time. The Metropolitan Opera in Lincoln Center, which was opened in 1966, has 3800 seats. San Francisco, which opened in 1932, has 3149. The Vienna *Staatsoper*, which was built in 1869, has 1709 (with 567 places for standing room). Venice's *La Fenice*, which was originally built in 1792, has 1126 seats. Not only do large theaters favor large orchestras; their size makes it harder to hear the words. In big houses, diction is less important than steady vocal production. It takes most of a singer's energy to fill the space. Lin-Manuel Miranda's *Hamilton* premiered in the Richard Rodgers Theater, which has 1400 seats. The audience heard every word. Not only was the theater small; the singers used amplification. Miranda knew the impact of *Hamilton* depended on the words as well as the music.

CHAPTER XIX

Lost and Found in Vienna

Das Ewig-Weibliche zieht uns hinan.
(The eternal feminine draws us upward.)

—JOHANN WOLFGANG GOETHE

WHEN I WAS NINETEEN, I LEFT STANFORD AFTER MY
freshman year to study in Vienna. I would like to claim
that I embarked on this adventure to pursue my destiny,
but I did it for a variety of bad reasons—including a girl.

I had come to Stanford expecting to find an intellectual home. For as long as I could remember, I had
yearned to be among my own kind. Instead, I found an
upscale version of my high school. The university had
carefully screened out the people I wanted to meet. Of
the twenty-one guys on my freshman corridor, seventeen had been student body president. The others were
an African American football player, a preppy from
Exeter, a physicist (whose father had worked on the
Manhattan Project), and me. The football player and I
were the only ones whose parents had not gone to college. I liked the ex-presidents—being likable was what
got them elected—and they liked me, but none of them
were my kind of people.

Coursework never gave me any problems, but I often seemed to be the only one who cared much about the books we were assigned. Stanford undergraduates were dutiful students, but they were too well-balanced to care about the arts and letters. In my first year I met no one who shared my interests. Surrounded by cordial people, I was lonely.

My instructors were uninspiring. They slogged or rambled through the material, but they were admirably demanding. They expected us to work, and we did. I dropped one course—in musical composition. After a few sessions, the professor met with me to ask about my preparation. He was pleased that I had twelve years of piano and five in woodwinds. When I told him that I had become fascinated by contemporary music in high school, he stiffened. He asked what composers I admired. With great pride—or perhaps vanity—I replied that my favorite living composers were Igor Stravinsky, Samuel Barber, Benjamin Britten, Aaron Copland, Michael Tippett, and William Walton. "Stravinsky is *gut*," he said in his Teutonic accent. "The others are *Quatsch!*" I had just learned that word in German. *Quatsch* meant nonsense, something too silly to be worth anyone's attention. "You must study Stockhausen, Boulez, and Berio," he declared. As he extolled their virtues, in particular their commitment to "total serialism" (the organization of all musical elements, including rhythm, dynamics, orchestral color, and pitch to a twelve-note series), I decided to find another course.

I liked many things about Stanford. I was especially enchanted by the calm beauty of the place. Stanford then was an uncluttered Romanesque-Revival campus set in eight thousand acres of mostly empty woodlands and sloping foothills. Santa Clara Valley was not yet Silicon Valley. It was still full of pastures and orchards. There were already a few changes. A giant radio telescope dominated one hilltop, but underneath it were grazing cattle.

I had never lived near open land. I had never lived anywhere that wasn't overbuilt and ugly. I walked for hours in the oak groves, lost in thought. The landscape filled me with joy. Yet I was never entirely at ease. Stanford's demi-Eden left me feeling alien and unworthy. I was an interloper. Amid such unaccustomed beauty, what else could I have done but fall hopelessly in love?

Hopeless romance expresses itself best in needless melodrama. On the last day of my unhappy freshman year, I discovered that a girl I had a desperate crush on was going to Europe in the fall. I did some quick research and discovered I could apply my California State Scholarship to a program Stanford ran in Vienna. I could study music there. I had already done a year of German. I was not a person who did things impulsively. Or so I thought. I just signed up. I wanted her and I wanted out.

My parents barely inquired about my change of plans. No one in my family had gone to college. They had no idea what it involved. Still overjoyed that I had made it into Stanford, my folks asked few questions about a world they found enigmatic. We had relatives in the Navy and Merchant Marine. They were always going overseas. Why not me?

When I arrived in Vienna three months later, in the fall of 1970, my putative romance was over. (Her doing—sigh—not mine.) Sad, lonely, and still a teenager, I had emotions to burn. I seethed, I slumped, I yearned. Some new passion was inevitable. I hoped it would be a girl.

I moved into a windowless room the size of a closet in a dreary *Studentenhaus*, run by Caritas, a Catholic charity. For months, I subsisted on a diet of solitude and self-pity. I made no friends. I hid in my room with a German dictionary reading Rilke, Brecht, and Goethe. (German may be the only language in which the poetry is easier than the prose.) I wasn't sure if I was waiting for a new life or just killing time.

No one visiting today's affluent and cosmopolitan Vienna will easily imagine the shadowy gray city I found in 1970. Vienna was still recovering from World War II. Injured veterans worked in newsstands and cigarette shops. Amputees begged in the train stations. Blind men tapped wooden canes along the sidewalk; at intersections strangers helped them cross the street. Every evening, around the corner from my residence, a dozen bedraggled prostitutes waited in doorways for clients. No longer wholly impoverished, the city was still barely getting by. Thrift, caution, and anxiety were everywhere apparent.

Having just arrived from 1960s California, the land

of endless sunshine and optimism, I wandered the dark streets and alleyways of the fallen imperial capital in a state of astonishment. I had stumbled into the film noir setting of *The Third Man*. An Angeleno abroad for the first time, I had never experienced the weight of history. A neutral country caught between Eastern and Western Europe, shorn of its empire, defeated in two murderous wars, complicit in the Holocaust, uncertain of its future, Austria clung to its glorious past with affection, pride, and desperation.

At the distance of so many years, I can't reconstruct my exact state of mind. The thoughts of youth are long, long thoughts. On my restless walks through the narrow cobblestone streets of the old city, I observed the trauma of people on the losing side of history. I hardly noticed how capably they had rebuilt their shattered society. I viewed their world through my own melancholy.

Vienna was an insular and self-contained metropolis. The city had its own way of doing everything, and those forms were meticulously observed. In Viennese parks, no one was allowed to step on the grass. Small formalities were important. Only minuscule tips were expected in cafés or taverns, but they had to be given in a particular way. Just walking down the street presented mysteries. Who were the small, filthy men carrying odd-shaped brooms—chimney sweeps, it turned out. Why did some men and women wear coats with green lapels? They were Tyroleans. Even the clothes looked different; not only the tailoring but the fabric had unfamiliar weaves and patterns. I let my hair grow long because the local barbers gave cuts that seemed boxy and bizarre to an American eye.

The food was varied and delicious, but it was drawn almost exclusively from the countries that had once made up the Austro-Hungarian Empire. There were morning and afternoon breaks for coffee and pastries, although some men had beer and wurst for their mid-morning snack. Language was a barrier. It wasn't just that few people spoke any English. The German was also a problem. The Viennese spoke their own dialect, *Wienerisch*, which was distinct from standard German. In every detail of daily life, an American experienced an overwhelming sense of foreignness—something no longer possible in today's generically international European capitals.

I arrived intending to be a composer. My residence was full of student musicians, both Austrian and foreign. On one floor there were three practice rooms each with a Bösendorfer grand piano, as well as a small recital hall with a fourth piano. I spent hours each day practicing and composing without any supervision while I also took courses in German and music. I had proficiency in three instruments but distinction in none. When I heard the other students rehearse, my heart sank. I would never be that good. I had training in music theory. I had taught myself basic orchestration. I had been composing since high school, but I had never put my whole energy into music. In Vienna, I realized that I was just an amateur. My love for music was greater than my talent.

Vienna had an extraordinary musical life. It was the one luxury the city could not live without. There were two major opera houses (plus a chamber opera company), two symphonies, numerous concerts, nightly recitals in several locations, and sung masses on Sunday, often with small orchestras. The movie theaters played opera films on weeknights. Classical music, especially the *Staatsoper* ("National Opera"), had the prominence there that major league baseball did in the U.S. I went to concerts and recitals several times a week, mostly to hear modern music. Many performances were free. Even the prestigious venues sold standing room—available an hour and fifteen minutes before each performance. I paid thirty-two cents to hear the *Wiener Symphoniker* and sixty cents at the *Staatsoper* to stand under the imperial box. (There were even cheaper tickets to stand in the balcony.) A restless teenager, I was as comfortable standing as sitting. I saw modern ballets and operas, but I avoided the standard repertory. I found traditional ballet too precious, I suffered through *Les Sylphides* three times so that I could see *Petrushka* after the intermission.

I loved hearing operatic music, but seeing full operas on stage was confusing. The stiff acting and staging added little enjoyment. The language barrier prevented me from knowing what was going on. As a senior in high school, I had won a statewide essay contest. On the trip to San Francisco to receive the award, I used part of my prize money to buy an orchestra seat to see *Die Walküre* with Regine Crespin and John Vickers. I loved parts of the music, but I was mostly bored. I could not experience the long work as theater. A few months later I saw *Falstaff* in Los Angeles with equal bewilderment. I liked modern opera, probably because I usually heard it in English.

Soon after my arrival, I decided to come to terms with the operatic Mozart. To do it properly, I bought the *Staatsoper*'s cheapest box seat for *Le Nozze di Figaro*. I found myself in the back seat of a box for five with only a partial view of the stage. My companions were an elderly quartet—three heavyset women in ancient gowns and a white-haired man in a threadbare tuxedo. He must have been married to one of the women; I couldn't tell which. For them, it was a grand occasion, a birthday or anniversary. They treated one another with elaborate courtesy. It was very sweet. If any woman stood, the man sprang from his seat to move her chair. Then he made a little bow.

Le Nozze is a long opera. I could only see one corner of the stage. I soon had no idea what was going on. If I stood for a moment to get a glimpse of the action, my box-mates reacted with horror. I'm embarrassed that what I remember most about the evening was how much the four old *Wieners* smelled. Few Viennese had bathrooms in their apartments. People visited the public baths perhaps once a week. In my back seat I was less conscious of Mozart's genius than the heady mix of body odor, heavy perfume, and mothballs. I was an antiseptic American, shocked by the atmosphere of *Mitteleuropa*. I left convinced that operas with powdered wigs and waistcoats were not for me. I would stick with modern music.

I would have stayed smugly in that benighted opinion had it not been for—what else draws men upward?—a girl. She was an American exchange student. When we met a few weeks later, she suggested we go to the opera. She was an attractive, intelligent, and determined young woman. As soon as we bought tickets for *La Bohème*, I realized her determination included a plan for our future. We would go to the opera, and I would fall in love.

Her plan worked. I fell in love that night but not with her. She had found good, cheap seats for a new Zeffirelli production. My music professors had been unanimous in dismissing Puccini. The mention of his name made their lips curl in the same sneer they gave to Rachmaninov and Sibelius. I had never heard much of Puccini's music beyond a few famous arias—mostly Miss America contestants singing *"Un bel di."* I expected something sentimental and obvious. I was unprepared for a masterpiece. At first, I was surprised by Puccini's masterful orchestration. Then the first great lyric scene began. By the time Rodolfo introduced himself to Mimi, I was in Puccini's thrall:

> *Chi son? Sono un poeta.*
> *Che cosa faccio? Scrivo.*
> *E come vivo? Vivo.*
> *In povertà mia lieta*
> *scialo da gran signore*
> *rime ed inni d'amore.*

[Who am I? I am a poet.
What do I do? I write.
How do I live? I survive.
In my happy poverty
Like a great lord, I squander
My love poems and rhymes.]

When the final curtain fell, I knew the young lady and I would never go out again. When you're aimless, it's best to drift alone. But I couldn't have imagined a better first date. To my own astonishment, I had fallen in love with opera—not just as disembodied music but as live theater. The experience had the suddenness and finality of destiny. Opera had always been there, waiting for me to sit in that seat on that evening.

Vienna had already introduced me to another intoxicating pleasure—drinking. I had been a priggish drinker before Europe. At a party I would cautiously nurse a beer all evening. I had seen too many drunks and drug addicts. In Vienna I learned to relax with fellow students in the city's picturesque taverns and wine cellars. I needed Austria's civilized attitude toward wine and beer. Alcohol has been a gift and never an addiction.

I cannot say the same thing about opera. It quickly became a far more alluring intoxication than alcohol. A few days after *La Bohème*, I went to see *Don Giovanni*— standing room, of course. Cesare Siepi and Sena Jurinac sang that night. I soaked it up. Whatever barrier I had experienced earlier vanished. I saw it again a few days later. I began going to the opera twice a week and then three or four times a week. I went to *Volksoper* to see different repertory, including *Porgy and Bess* with an African American cast that included William Warfield. By then, I had a few friends. I convinced them to come to the opera. Each of them came once. Not all pleasures need to be social. I enjoyed a luxury of seeing the same opera repeatedly in the same season with different casts. It is an indulgence I've never been able to afford in America. Going to the *Staatsoper* three times a week cost me less than two dollars.

The physical productions in Vienna were uneven. The scenery of *Don Giovanni* consisted mostly of canvas backdrops. *The Magic Flute* had a beautiful and elaborate set. The music, however, was consistently superb. The Vienna Philharmonic was in the pit, and the regular singers would now seem like a gala cast. Along with Siepi and Jurinac were Wilma Lipp, Anton Dermota, Gundula Janowitz, Giuseppe Taddei, Peter Schreier, and Wolfgang Windgassen. For special performances, Franco Corelli, Leontyne Price, Birgit Nilsson, René Kollo, and other stars would arrive. I haven't written much about singers because that subject lies outside my focus, but let me state the obvious. Opera exists only through the skill and artistry of singers. I didn't understand opera until I saw great singers perform it.

During the days, I immersed myself in German. It was the language of both my studies and of the city around me. I began to dream in German, which I found unsettling. Now that English had little to do with both my daily life and dream world, I heard it differently. My native tongue acquired a magical power, evoking powerful memories and imaginative associations. I began reading poetry obsessively and bought overpriced paperbacks of modern verse at the city's one English-language bookstore.

I had always liked poetry, but I had never studied it seriously. I certainly had never thought of myself as a poet. I filled two small notebooks with verse. I liked playing with language. The little academic instruction I'd had treated the poem as a written text to be analyzed visually on the page. That approach seemed backwards. It was the sound of poetry that attracted me. It wasn't a mute and immobile art like a painting or sculpture. Poetry was a kind of song—it was sound moving through time. The printed page was just a score waiting for a performance. As I worked in my notebook, I noticed that most of what I had learned about music applied to verse. A rhythm could make an ordinary sentence memorable. A phrase could take the expressive shape of a melody.

Occasionally, I wrote a good line by accident, but I never wrote a passable poem. Failure didn't bother me. I was a kid feeling out the keys of a piano. Music had taught me that mastery took years of study and effort. I had loved the art but not the effort. But poetry was different. The prospect of undertaking that enormous effort excited me.

One day I woke up and knew I would be a poet. The moment was without drama. My vocation arrived quietly as a *fait accompli*. I didn't choose the art. It chose me. I simply assented. If I felt anything, it was relief. I hardly understood what the decision meant, but I knew it was permanent. Since then, I have rejoiced in it and have cursed it. I have never doubted it.

Vienna taught me many things. The most important was the futility of planning the future too carefully. I came to Austria as a composer. I left as a poet. I didn't abandon music; I followed it somewhere unexpected. It brought me into poetry by a different avenue from my contemporaries. And that, as Robert Frost observed, can make all the difference. Stranger still, years later poetry led me back to music as a lyricist and librettist. Hofmannsthal's Marschallin is right, *Die Zeit, die ist ein sonderbar Ding.* So many things you strive for—like love—suddenly fail. Then some unexpected gift—like opera—appears in its place. Even bad luck has its advantages. It makes room for serendipity. I lost two girlfriends but found the Muse.

CHAPTER XX

Bernstein's Broken Promise

*Musicals are, by nature, theatrical, meaning
poetic, meaning having to move the audience's
imagination and create a suspension of disbelief.*

—STEPHEN SONDHEIM

THE YOUNG LEONARD BERNSTEIN APPEARED IDEALLY
suited to create a new vernacular form of American
opera. A musical polymath, he stood as the successor
to Gershwin and Copland, composers who had combined classical and popular material to create serious
but accessible theatrical works of dance and opera.
Bernstein was a composer equally at home in the symphony hall and Broadway theater with a special genius
for both vocal music and modern dance.

Bernstein began his operatic career with distinction. His first opera, the one-act *Trouble in Tahiti* (1952),
for which the composer wrote his own sharp and effective lyrics, was a bittersweet *tour de force*. The short
opera moves with such speed and self-assurance that
it is easy to underestimate its brilliance. It has a fully
developed and original style—a fusion of Broadway
melody and orchestral dynamism unlike any earlier

American opera. Compared to the awkward first works of other operatic masters, such as Verdi's *Oberto*, Puccini's *Le Villi*, or Strauss's *Guntram*, Bernstein's debut piece seems preternaturally fluent and accomplished. One hears a personal voice handled confidently and consistently from start to finish.

Of course, Bernstein was not a novice to theatrical music. He had already composed two ballets (*Fancy Free* and *Facsimile*) as well as two musicals (*On the Town* and *Peter Pan*). He appeared to move into opera effortlessly, tightening his style without losing his musical personality. *Trouble in Tahiti* has enormous wit and vivacity with one memorable number after another. The opera depicts a suburban couple—Sam and Dinah—ostensibly in love who gradually recognize the loneliness and isolation within their marriage. The musical climax is the soprano's hilarious account of the "terrible, awful movie" she has just seen titled *Trouble in Tahiti*. Gradually her ridicule becomes suffused with her own longing for the adventure and romance her suburban life denies.

Although broadcast on NBC television, *Trouble in Tahiti* did not attain the popularity the composer and producers expected, especially after the huge success of Menotti's *Amahl and the Night Visitors* a few months earlier. Bernstein's doomed vision of marriage did not sit well with prime-time viewers. It is either ironic or revelatory that Bernstein composed much of the work on the honeymoon of his long and troubled marriage with Felicia Montealegre. Thirty years later he revised and expanded the opera into *A Quiet Place* (1983). This lugubrious three-act muddle begins at Dinah's funeral where the family descends into anger, recrimination, and guilt. The original opera appears as a flashback. *A Quiet Place* underwent two revisions with Bernstein eventually chopping *Trouble in Tahiti* into two pieces for the second act. Nothing could save the long, depressing psychodrama. It took a lot to smother the tight and tuneful *Trouble in Tahiti*, but *A Quiet Place* managed. Its failure to cohere was a microcosm of Bernstein's late career when the weight of his international success as a conductor, teacher, and media celebrity, aggravated by his worsening health, made ambitious compositions impossible.

Things had looked brighter in 1957 when Bernstein strengthened his position as the great hope of American opera with *West Side Story*, an inspired fusion of theatrical song and modern dance. The musical was breathtaking in its originality. Based on Shakespeare's *Romeo and Juliet*, set among teenage gangs in the slums soon to be cleared to erect Lincoln Center, *West Side Story* was a work of self-consciously high ambition. The songs, book, and choreography were more carefully integrated than other shows of the period. The piece even risked a tragic ending, a rare thing in commercial musical theater. Many listeners compare its high points to opera—indeed the songs are now frequently performed by opera stars—but *West Side Story* was firmly rooted in Broadway with indelible lyrics by the young Stephen Sondheim and the expressive choreography of Jerome Robbins. It isn't just the dialogue that makes the work feel awkward in an opera house. *West Side Story* was designed for a versatile company of young theatrical singer-dancers. The choreography was as important as the songs in driving the narrative. Imagine the Met's male chorus snapping their fingers as they stomped through "When You're a Jet." The audience would put their money on the Sharks. Some consider *West Side Story* the best Broadway musical of all time. No one would rank it far from the top. Bernstein was not yet forty. Surely a great opera was in his future.

Bernstein wrote his only other opera by accident. His musical *Candide* (1956) had a book by Lillian Hellman and lyrics by Richard Wilbur (with some earlier material by John Latouche and Dorothy Parker). *Candide* opened in a strong production directed by Tyrone Guthrie, but the expensive show was a box office disaster closing after two months. The failure puzzled its creators. Everyone knew it didn't work, but they also recognized the show was full of wonderful things. Fixing *Candide* didn't prove easy. There would be ten revised versions before the work settled into its final form. Hellman's serious and political book was replaced by a lighter, shorter script by Hugh Wheeler. Bernstein and Wilbur added new songs.

Despite several early revisions, the musical still failed to achieve the proper momentum for a Broadway show, but it worked when opera companies produced it. Opera audiences brought different expectations to

Candide than did theatergoers. Eventually an opera-house version was crafted by many hands, including Stephen Sondheim. More dialogue was cut, some lyrics sharpened, and nearly every musical number or cue was included—old, new, and previously discarded. As Sondheim remarked in another context, "Musical comedies aren't written, they are rewritten." After forty-three years of revisions, the final and successful operatic version consisted mostly of songs and ensembles. As it turned out, the problem had always been in the libretto, specifically the book. It wasn't just Hellman's wordy original but all the conventional Broadway prose dialogue. What audiences loved were the clever songs. Prose had doomed *Candide* until poetry saved it.

Porgy and Bess and *Candide* are both number operas with spoken dialogue. Although they contain stretches of orchestral music—*Porgy* has a great deal of symphonic scene-setting—neither has a continuous score. The individual numbers propel the dramatic structure. Mainstream opera companies would probably have been suspicious of the approach. A number opera would have seemed insufficiently serious for classical music unless it was employed with self-conscious irony as in Auden and Kallman's deliberately archaic libretto for Igor Stravinsky's *The Rake's Progress.*

It is not coincidental that both *Porgy* and *Candide* emerged from commercial theater. Broadway has a different way of developing musical theater. It puts greater emphasis on the lyrics than opera companies do. It is worth noting that five of the ten most widely performed American operas premiered not in an opera house but in commercial theater or on television. That is an astonishing and significant fact for an art form that exists entirely in the non-profit sector, supported more by private and public donations than box office receipts.

Commercial theater understands something that opera companies do not—the expressive power of strong and memorable lyrics. The talent needed to compose an expressive melody is self-evident, but writing lyrics demands great skill, too—a quirky genius that even poets rarely possess. It is not a talent most playwrights have, which is why Broadway usually selects different authors for the book and lyrics. When a lyricist perfectly matches words to a melody, people feel it.

Anyone who hears *Porgy and Bess* or *Candide* in an opera house notices how the audience's engagement changes. It isn't merely a matter of hearing the words in English. Audiences don't listen to the text of Britten's *Turn of the Screw* with the same sort of attention, even though it has a fine libretto. Music alone doesn't deliver the same theatrical effect. Aaron Copland's *The Tender Land* has a beautiful score, characteristic of the composer at his best, but Erik Johns's book and lyrics are so corny they make the crowd wince. (When *The Tender Land* premiered in 1954, the New York City Opera pulled it after three performances.) With *Porgy* and *Candide* operagoers respond to the poetic power of lyrics meant to be heard line by line. They are enchanted by the power of song.

CHAPTER XXI

Opera and Song

Gesang ist Dasein.
(Singing is being.)

—RAINER MARIA RILKE

SONG HAS AN EXISTENTIAL STATUS THAT CLASSICAL MUSI-
cians sometimes forget. It no longer seems to have much
connection to what serious composers do. To classically
trained contemporary composers, song is an inferior or
negligible category, amateur music that lacks sophistication and complexity. How can anyone compare
modern opera to teenagers in a garage band? This professional bias isn't arbitrary. It is a reasonable response
to the gross commercialization of song in a media-
saturated culture. That is a world which classical artists
now define themselves against. Nonetheless it is important to see song from a broader perspective—not as a
commercial category but as an essential human behav-
ior. Song isn't a thirty-two-bar musical form. It is a primal mode of human communication and communality.

Song is a universal human art. No one has found
a culture which does not have song. It is also a ubiq-
uitous art—used for every human activity from wor-

ship to warfare. Armies once sang as they marched off to battle. Sailors chanted as they put out to sea. Shepherds sang to their flocks. Mothers still sing to their sleepy children. Whether solo or choral, song is communal. It links the singer to the listener. Song can be stylized and developed in countless ways from bel canto to Kabuki, but the underlying common impulse remains. Song is magical. The Latin word for song is *carmen*, a word that also means a poem, magical spell, or prophecy. All poetry was originally sung. Its purpose was to enchant, seduce, comfort, and include. Songs are spells to awaken and enlarge emotions—listeners weep or smile, they feel affinity or loss. Songs communicate across languages. People feel meaning in songs whose words they don't understand.

Song isn't intellectual. It communicates physically and holistically. But song is most powerful when the listener understands and feels each word memorably reinforced by both the music and the human voice that performs it. There is a reason that Orpheus has appeared in opera since its origins. The first poet, he created songs that transformed nature and moved the gods of death to compassion. Ezra Pound declared, "Music rots when it gets too far from dance. Poetry atrophies when it gets too far from music." Opera was created to reunite song and poetry to recapture that primal magic. Opera abandons song at great risk.

Orchestral opera has one sort of special power. Works such as *Parsifal* or *Pelléas et Mélisande* immerse the audience in the mood and emotions of the drama.

The continuous flow of music carries the listener forward according to the composer's design. Philip Glass channels this power in his epic operas. In *Akhnaten*, the words matter less than the shimmering sound of the orchestra and chorus. (The music pulses with dance-rhythms, slow and fast, that Pound would have admired.) Overwhelmed by *son et lumière*, the audience hardly cares that the libretto is in ancient Egyptian, Aramaic, Hebrew, and Akkadian. Glass has the old-fashioned theatrical instinct, however, to end the middle act with "Hymn to the Sun," a rhapsodic aria sung in English (or the language of the audience). The self-contained musical number creates a human connection between the title character and the listener. The aria is the most popular moment in the three-hour work. Although *Akhnaten* has spoken narration, no critic has dared to call it an operetta. Like *The Magic Flute*, whose Masonic episodes it resembles, the work is too serious to demote.

Number operas achieve their enchantment in a different way—not as a continuous line of sound but a series of rising and falling motions. Each musical number creates a self-contained moment of expressive power. Different numbers seek different effects. Together they build an overall dramatic plan. Lyrics play a crucial role in establishing the nature of each new number. No Italian baritone singing *"Largo al factotum"* from Rossini's *Barber of Seville* will slur the words; they are clever and amusing, even to foreigners. Singers revel in their power to enthrall a crowd. Figaro's monologue is witty, rhythmic, and well rhymed. In Rossini's frenetic setting, it becomes unforgettable. Even Bugs Bunny can bring it off. The aria's climax, when the barber's many clients simultaneously call for his services, requires no translation to make itself felt:

Figaro qua, Figaro la,
Figaro su, Figaro giu.
Pronto prontissimo son come il fulmine,
Sono il factotum della città.

Librettist Cesare Sterbini is not remembered as one of opera's great laureates, but it would be a mistake to underestimate his talent. Figaro's exuberant entrance aria has no parallel or precedent in either of Sterbini's sources, Pierre Beaumarchais's play, *Le Barbier de Séville* (1775) or Giovanni Paisiello's opera, *Il Barbiere di Siviglia* (1782). The show-stopping number was Sterbini's invention. His rapid-fire lyrics not only inspired Rossini's most famous aria; they trigger the scene's madcap comedy. Farce requires immense sophistication. *"Largo al factotum"* is an explosion of lyrical self-assertion that joyfully interrupts the drama—an effect a through-composed score cannot easily duplicate. Opera is richer for having both styles.

CHAPTER XXII

Operatic Sondheim

If I'm going to sing like somebody else,
then I don't need to sing at all.

—BILLIE HOLIDAY

STEPHEN SONDHEIM'S WORK REPRESENTS THE CULMINA-
tion of the quest to create a new American opera from
popular musical theater. More than Bernstein or even
Gershwin, two of his formative influences, Sondheim
developed a mode of musical and poetical composition
that gave his later shows a unified style and continuous
momentum without losing the power of their individual numbers. His fusion of popular energy and classical cohesion endowed his best work, especially *Sweeney
Todd*, with a dynamic lyricality and broad appeal that
no classical American opera composer of his generation could match.

In American musical theater, Sondheim is a figure
as singular as Wagner was to Romantic opera. Conventional assumptions don't account for his career. Blessed
with a rare combination of musical and literary talent,
which had been trained since childhood, Sondheim

controlled the course of his own artistic development. He found the creative and financial support for his innovative ventures, despite many failures. By forty, he had become the most influential creative artist in American musical theater, a position he held for another half century. Like Wagner, he spawned many imitators, all inferior to the original. Sondheim can only be understood on his own terms. He was the exception who disproved the rules.

Sondheim embodied the most sophisticated traditions of American musical theater. He was both to the manner and the manor born. At the age of ten, the privileged, lonely boy fell under the tutorship of his next-door neighbor, Oscar Hammerstein II. The lyricist became an informal foster-father and guided the young songwriter for two decades until his death. "I was essentially trained by Oscar Hammerstein," Sondheim recalled, "to think of songs as one-act plays, to move a song from point A to point B dramatically." In his early twenties, Sondheim worked as the lyricist for Leonard Bernstein's *West Side Story* and Jule Styne's *Gypsy*, two landmark musicals. In 1962, Sondheim mounted his first show as both composer and lyricist, *A Funny Thing Happened on the Way to the Forum*. Modeled on the Latin comedies of Plautus, the musical had an innocent and irresistible silliness Sondheim would never recapture. It won six Tonys (including the top prize for Best Musical). Ironically, it also had the longest Broadway run of any Sondheim show over his long career. That must have rankled in his later years. But, as Goethe observed, to be lucky at the start is everything for an artist.

A Funny Thing was an inspired but conventional musical. In his subsequent work, Sondheim reinvented, show by show, the style and structure of the American musical. He not only changed the form of theatrical lyrics but also their themes. Working in collaboration with a changing cast of dramatists who wrote his books, he played Modernist games with narrative. In *Company* (1970), he replaced the plotline with a series of loosely connected vignettes. In *Follies* (1971), former showgirls gather in a theater scheduled for demolition where they are joined by the ghosts of their younger selves to relive their disappointments and dance routines. In *Merrily We Roll Along* (1981), the story is told backwards. These narrative tricks had the effect of removing the typical emotional arc of a Broadway show. Instead, they created a Brechtian *Verfremdungseffekt*, a distancing effect, that prevents the audience from easily identifying with the characters (who are usually busy observing themselves). Needless to say, clinical detachment was not the feeling commercial musicals are supposed to deliver.

Sondheim's formal experimentation continued in idiosyncratic works such as *Pacific Overtures* (1976), *Sunday in the Park with George* (1984), and *Assassins* (1990), which had plots and themes that had nothing in common with traditional musicals. Each was inspired, original, but ultimately unsatisfactory, though Sondheim's misses were generally more interesting than the successes of his Broadway contemporaries. Meanwhile as a composer, he devised ingenious ways to connect his songs and dialogue with nearly continuous orchestral accompaniment. In *Sweeney Todd* (1979) and *Into the Woods* (1987), he pushed the boundaries of the musical until it seemed to merge into opera.

Significantly, Sondheim's innovation was done within the constraints of commercial theater. (One can't say "for-profit theater" without irony since so many of his shows lost money.) Sondheim never wanted to be anywhere except in the marketplace. He accepted its limitations as the necessary price to obtain its resources of talent, expertise, and money. Broadway was the only place he could work at the level of his ambition. Sondheim took pride in his hits and accepted his flops with stoic detachment. Failure stung, but he respected the authority of the audience; these people had allowed him to be a serious artist in a commercial category. Sondheim rejected the supposed polarity between high and low culture. He dismissed classical composer Ned Rorem's condescending remarks about popular song. "You make a mistake," Sondheim declared, "when you divide things into serious and pop." His artistic achievement rested on his refusal to make the division everyone else took for granted.

There is no need to argue for Sondheim's creative eminence. He was the major American theatrical composer of the last half century. Without including *West Side Story* or *Gypsy*, at least six of his shows remain actively in the repertory—*A Funny Thing, Company, Follies, A Little Night Music, Sweeney Todd,* and *Into the*

Woods. That is about the same number as the Rodgers and Hammerstein works still performed (though Sondheim's shows had shorter runs, fewer movies, and almost no major hit songs). He won eight Tonys, eight Grammy Awards, an Academy Award, a Pulitzer Prize, and the National Medal of Arts.

Sondheim's long-standing preeminence leads people to forget how often he failed. Half of his shows flopped, including *Anyone Can Whistle*, *Do I Hear a Waltz?*, *Assassins*, and *Road Show*. Other projects were abandoned. Some shows, such as *Follies*, *Passion*, and *Pacific Overtures* enjoyed only modest success and lost money for their investors. Even his hits never matched the box office appeal of down-market fare such as *Chicago*, *The Producers*, or *Wicked*. A list of the 124 longest-running Broadway shows does not include a single Sondheim score. Yet he wasn't a coterie composer. One might say he captured half the audience, not a bad percentage for an artist. His shows, he observed, provoked "polarized reactions of fervent admiration or ferocious rejection." But his admirers included the serious theatrical crowd—led by critics who knew from the first that he was a major figure.

Sondheim's critical reputation requires no tune-up. He occupies a permanent place in American theater. The relevant question here is whether that place includes opera. Did Sondheim ever write a real opera? It is not an idle question since it affects the understanding of what American opera is and what cultural resources best nourish it. To answer the question, it helps to see

Sondheim's career in the context of theatrical history. During his seventy-year professional life, the American musical lost its influential position in popular culture. As he remarked about songwriting:

> It used to be that the musical theater was the source of popular music. It's no longer true . . . Nowadays, artists write their own songs, for the most part—artists meaning singers. That has freed the composers of musical theater. They don't have to write in the standard forms.

Beginning in the 1960s, popular music developed in ways that had little to do with the Tin Pan Alley songwriters who had dominated theatrical, broadcast, and movie music since the turn of the century. Rock, Soul, Country, and other styles became the commercial mainstream. Pop artists increasingly wrote their own material. The cultural and economic shift hurt theatrical songwriters, but it also liberated them, if they were up to the challenge. The better Broadway musicals, like opera a century earlier, moved from simpler song forms to more complicated ones. Sondheim was the prime mover of the change. He was the monarch of a shrinking kingdom.

Sondheim's early works had been traditional book-driven shows with discrete songs and ensembles separated by dialogue. *A Funny Thing*'s opening number, "Comedy Tonight," is ancient Rome's version of Irving Berlin's "There's No Business Like Show Business." Both numbers can be excerpted and successfully performed in new contexts. As Sondheim developed more complex and individual forms of songwriting, he began to write numbers that could not easily be extracted from the shows; they were too deeply lodged in the complicated personalities of his characters. *Company* and *Follies* both won the Tony for Best Musical, but neither left hit songs. Compared to the previous generation of Broadway songwriters, such as Rodgers and Hammerstein, Lerner and Loewe, or Comden and Green, Sondheim's huge catalogue of songs is noteworthy for its lack of crossover success. The single notable exception was the wistful but enigmatic "Send in the Clowns" from *A Little Night Music*, which was popularized by Frank Sinatra and Judy Collins. To work independently of his show, his songs require the intimacy of cabaret. Sondheim is less like Jerome Kern than Franz Schubert; he became the art-song composer of Broadway. Lieder recitals of Sondheim songs have become standard fare, especially for small theaters.

Each Sondheim show in his middle period explored new musical and thematic areas. *A Little Night Music* (1973), based on Ingmar Bergman's film comedy, *Smiles of a Summer Night*, was written mostly in waltz time. Witty, sophisticated, and discreetly risqué, it resembled a classic operetta, a form that had been moribund since Franz Lehár and Sigmund Romberg. The show became a reverse crossover hit; it didn't move forward into pop culture but backwards into the high-art world of opera. The 1977 movie, with Elizabeth Taylor miscast in the leading role, was a critical and box office bomb, but opera companies began producing the show successfully to full houses and strong reviews.

Next came one of Sondheim's oddest but most beguiling shows, *Pacific Overtures* (1976), an alternately satiric and poetic chronicle of Japanese history. Performed in mock-Kabuki style by an all-male Asian cast, it depicted the arrival of the American fleet in 1853 to westernize Japan. Despite one of Sondheim's best scores and a striking production, the show failed. The episodic book and arresting individual songs never cohered. Like several of Sondheim's weaker shows, the second act of *Pacific Overtures* flagged and meandered. (It often proved difficult for Sondheim to sustain the ingenious premises with which his shows opened.) Yet *Pacific Overtures* contained several numbers, such as "Chrysanthemum Tea," "Welcome to Kanagawa," and "Someone in a Tree" that rank among Sondheim's most remarkable compositions. They demonstrated his growing mastery of extended vocal scenes and ensembles. Complicated to produce and rarely revived, *Pacific Overtures* belongs to the category of shows best experienced as a soundtrack album.

Much of Sondheim's artistic evolution was poetic. In the six years from *Follies* to *Pacific Overtures*, Sondheim established a new tone for the American musical—verbally dazzling, conceptually bold, and emotionally cool. His early lyrics for Bernstein and Styne had been smart, self-assured, and clever; he was writing for someone else's show. The lyrics of *Company* and *Follies* were more personal; they stayed clever but also grew anxious, introspective, and detached. *Follies* had a world-weariness only a metrosexual hitting forty can manage. These were not feel-good shows. Hammerstein and Lerner lyrics delivered warmth, charm, and romance. Sondheim offered witty ballads of ambivalence, anxiety, and disappointment.

There had been sad songs on Broadway before Sondheim, but few that offered no solution for that sadness. Even in *A Little Night Music*, Sondheim's most optimistic show since *A Funny Thing*, there was a constant note of despair:

> Every day a little death
> In the parlor, in the bed,
> In the curtains, in the silver,
> In the buttons, in the bread.
> Every day a little sting,
> In the heart and in the head,
> Every move and every breath,
> And you hardly feel a thing,
> Brings a perfect little death.

Sondheim's signature characters are alert, articulate, and disenchanted. However much they long for love and fulfilment, they no longer believe in happy endings. Ambivalent about their own lives, they are, by turns, tender, bemused, and bitter.

The emotional detachment of Sondheim's lyrics, more than his musical or dramatic experimentalism, was the element that polarized his audience. Broadway had specialized in selling the public musical romance; Sondheim offered them fatalistic realism. Instead of *Schmalz* he gave them *Weltschmerz*. Romance shows us the world as we wish it could be; realism reveals the confusion and disappointments of existence. Sondheim's lyrics exploit the ironies and incongruities when great expectations become lost illusions.

No lesser poet could have managed this difficult stance with such success. If Sondheim disturbed his audience, he also never failed to charm it. His disconcerting songs expressed themselves in clever turns of phrase made memorable by pointed rhymes. Alienation had never seemed more stylish. Yet even Sondheim had missteps. In *Company*, for example, the first act closed with a bittersweet and tentative love song, "Marry Me a Little."

> Marry me a little,
> Love me just enough.
> Cry, but not too often,
> Play, but not too rough.
> Keep a tender distance,
> So we'll both be free.

The song was cut from the original production, then reinstated in some revivals; finally it became the title number of an off-Broadway revue of Sondheim songs dropped from his musicals. Why did such a simple and urbane song cause such distress? Any listener knows it proposed a doomed relationship.

Musicals are the most extroverted form of theater, perhaps of all literature. In the boisterous company of Broadway's major songwriters, Sondheim seems temperamentally out of place—a poet among entertainers, an introvert among exhibitionists. Sondheim often intensified the dissonance and detachment of his lyrics by framing them in assertive theatrical concepts. Having a plot move backwards or dramatizing the creation of a Post-Impressionist masterpiece makes a show distinctive and surprising. Such novelty can also obscure its emotional content. As John Simon complained about Sondheim (and concept shows in general), they were "clever rather than penetrating, revealing, exhilarating, moving." That criticism may not be entirely true, but neither is it entirely false. Audiences have to think their way through some Sondheim shows; not everyone appreciates the experience.

By now, diehard Sondheim fans will be thoroughly annoyed. While my admiration for the songwriter is clear, my coverage has included serious qualifications and criticisms. Why not just accept everything Sondheim wrote with gratitude and stop the carping and complaint? I have described the songwriter's early career critically to clarify the special qualities of his finest later shows—*A Little Night Music*, *Sweeney Todd*, and *Into the Woods*. Different from the works that gave him his first celebrity, they reflect Sondheim's deepening sense of himself as a composer, lyricist, and dramatist. They represented a creative breakthrough that produced shows as ambitious and original as any of his early works but also, *pace* Simon, more moving, revelatory, and exhilarating.

The narrative structures of the three later shows have more clarity and solidity than the experiments of the middle period. The plots also have stronger closure. One might even say that each show ends happily in its own way. The romantic couples sort themselves out successfully in *A Little Night Music.* In *Sweeney Todd* the title character gets the revenge he desires, and the young lovers escape danger. *Into the Woods* has two happy endings, one for each act, though the second finale comes at great cost. Significantly, the three musicals are set in historical periods or fantasy, not in contemporary New York City. The characters cross class lines and age groups. The motivations of the main figures are clear—love, sex, wealth, respect, revenge. There is still great nuance in characterization, but there is also vitality. The inner drama remains, but it resolves itself in decisive external actions, often violent or farcical. Sondheim's sensibility still pervades each work, but there is greater range of tone and theme since he has been emancipated from writing about his own life and milieu.

Sondheim's music reflects this new freedom. It becomes more ample and intricate, and unrestrained in its lyricality. There is less spoken dialogue and more *parlando*—singing that imitates speech patterns. The scores have more continuous orchestral underpinning. The music is still rooted in popular musical theater, but the treatment becomes increasingly operatic. One saw Sondheim struggling toward this new fluid style in *Pacific Overtures*. It expands in *A Little Night Music*, most notably in the concertized, first act finale, "A Weekend in the Country." But its perfection comes in *Sweeney Todd*, Sondheim's masterpiece.

Sweeney Todd has an odd and disreputable genealogy. The story of the "Demon Barber of Fleet Street" originates in a penny dreadful novel serialized in the winter of 1846–47. The tale was quickly brought to the popular stage. George Dibdin Pitt's *The String of Pearls, or the Fiend of Fleet Street* opened in London before the final episode of the magazine serial was published. In 1970, Christopher Bond adapted the melodrama for a weightier play, which provides the title character with a cogent backstory and motivation for his crimes. Sondheim saw the musical potential of Bond's play. He enlarged the cast and scope. The tawdry Victorian shocker differed from any plot he had used before— more violent, raucous, and dark. Sondheim had always cultivated a bleak tone in his lyrics, but the unpleasant emotions were internalized, sublimated, and tamed. The characters in *Sweeney Todd* are not paralyzed by introspection, they are ready to act at the right moment, usually without moral scruple or remorse.

The primal terror and cruel comedy of *Sweeney Todd* broadened Sondheim's artistic range. The cool and detached lyricist wrote songs of uninhibited and dangerous emotion. He also crafted a macabre sound to animate his "musical horror story." The orchestra eventually included both an organ and a shrieking factory

whistle to achieve its unnerving effects. There is surprising variety in the tightly unified score with numbers unlike anything in earlier shows. Who would have
predicted that one of Sondheim's funniest songs, "A Little Priest," would be in praise of cannibalism? As Tim
Page commented, the work "is both genuinely funny
and genuinely terrifying."

Not the least of Sondheim's accomplishments in
Sweeney Todd was his compelling and original solution
to the oldest operatic dilemma—what does a composer
do about all the dialogue drama requires? The question of how to set dialogue has been central to operatic style since the form's invention in 1598. The first
operas made little distinction between what we would
now call song and dialogue. All of the words were
chanted expressively with frequent ornamentation. In
the Baroque and Classical periods composers set dialogue perfunctorily as recitative—quickly sung words
that follow speech rhythms. This rapid, no-nonsense
dialogue allowed the singers and audiences to get expe-
diently to what they loved best—the full-throated singing. No one ever came to the opera for the recitatives.
They gave little pleasure; they just kept the drama moving, at least for Italians. Foreign audiences endured
them in polite bewilderment.

Since Mozart, composers have explored different
ways of integrating expository dialogue into the musical structure of the score. Wagner created a continuous orchestral base over which monologue or dialogue
could be sung. In the second act of *Die Walküre*, to give

an extreme example, Wotan stands holding his spear for nine minutes narrating his backstory while the orchestra stews and roils with leitmotifs. It is no one's favorite moment. In Italy composers gradually replaced the recitatives with *arioso*, "airy" speech, more melodic than declamatory but not quite an aria. Modern composers developed new techniques. Schoenberg and Berg used rhythmic speech in rising and falling pitches (*Sprechstimme*) which has a striking expressive effect. Orff and Glanville-Hicks employed a sinuous chant accompanied only by simple bass harmonies. Barber and Menotti favored *arioso*. Weill and Gershwin kept spoken dialogue. Poulenc, Britten, and Henze used a little of everything.

Broadway shows had traditionally been content to have performers stop talking and then suddenly burst into song. There were a few notable experiments—such as Meredith Willson's extraordinary "Rock Island Railroad" number that opened *The Music Man* (1957). A group of traveling salesman argue in highly accented speech to the accelerating rhythms of the train.

> Cash for the merchandise, cash for the button hooks,
> Cash for the cotton goods, cash for the hard goods,
> Cash for the fancy goods, cash for the soft goods,
> Cash for the noggins and the piggins and the firkins,
> Cash for the hogshead, cask and demijohn.
> Cash for the crackers and the pickles and the flypaper
> Look, whadaya talk, whadaya talk, whadaya talk,
>   whadaya talk, whadaya talk?

There is no singing. The speech is hammered in rhythmic patterns—an episode now recognized as prefiguring hip-hop. Schoenberg never wrote *Sprechstimme* half so lively. No one followed Willson's lead. Broadway happily continued to alternate dialogue and song.

Sondheim composed *Sweeney Todd* as a nearly continuous score. Eighty percent of the text is set to music. He uses nearly every technique from the musical and operatic traditions—full song, *arioso*, declamation, and melodrama (words spoken over orchestral accompaniment) to integrate the songs and dialogue. There is also a stark choral presence. The orchestra pushes the drama forward, sometimes brutally. Everything is, in Sondheim's words, "held together by ceaseless underpinning." The effect is emotionally overwhelming. From the first, critics and audiences saw the work's resemblance to opera.

Sondheim was slyly evasive when journalists asked him if *Sweeney Todd* was an opera. He mentioned his "antipathy to opera." Sometimes he gave a curt response, *Sweeney Todd* was a "dark operetta" or "movie for the stage." More often he gave a philosophical response. His epistemology was simple:

> There's a philosophy that says the object changes in terms of how it's viewed . . . It's how it's received by the audience that changes the whole color, changes the relationship of the performers onstage to the audience—which is the necessary part of a theater experience.

This perspective led Sondheim to respond to queries with two conditional statements. First, if his work was done in an opera house, it was an opera; if it was performed in a theater, it was a musical. Second, if his piece is sung by operatic voices, it was an opera; if it was sung by theatrical voices, it was a musical. Each tradition performed the work according to its own standards, and each audience viewed the work from its own perspective. Having seen *Sweeney Todd* in both contexts, I can testify to both its general appeal and duality. The work is sung and heard differently in each venue; yet the result is always enthusiastic acceptance.

When critics argue about the operatic status of *Sweeney Todd*, they usually raise three objections: it has spoken dialogue; it can be sung by non-operatic voices; it is rooted in Broadway traditions. All of these statements are true, but none convincingly disqualify it.

Sweeney Todd indeed has dialogue, about the same amount as *The Magic Flute*, *Fidelio*, or *Carmen*. Sondheim's score establishes the dramatic structure; it incorporates the words, sung or spoken, into a unified musical design. There are over thirty numbers in *Sweeney Todd*, the most of any Sondheim show, as well as opening and closing choruses. Much of the spoken dialogue is set over orchestral accompaniment. Speech also alternates with singing for theatrical effect. In performance, *Sweeney Todd* has the steady musical momentum of an opera rather than the episodic feeling of a musical or operetta. No one doubts the operatic status of *Fidelio* or *The Magic Flute*, despite their dialogue, because the music is too magnificent for a *Singspiel*. *Sweeney Todd* sounds nothing like Beethoven or Mozart, but, superb in its own way, its music moves with unmistakable gravity and authority. If *Fidelio* and *The Magic Flute* are operas, so is *Sweeney Todd*. Opera is a more inclusive form than purists claim.

The vocal argument against Sondheim is parochial. *Sweeney Todd* is not a score for amateurs, but it can be sung by actors with trained theatrical voices. The work can also be sung to greater effect by operatic voices. Is that versatility a fault? Operatic voices are highly specialized. No soprano can sing all of the soprano repertory. A coloratura can't safely manage heavy dramatic roles such as Brunnhilde or Elektra; Wagnerian sopranos likewise have difficulty singing bel canto roles such as Lucia or Amina. There are many types of operatic voices. Voices are sorted early and trained to realize the different styles of music across the repertory from Monteverdi to Messiaen.

Isn't Broadway singing, which favors chest voice over head voice and emphasizes clear diction, just another sort of specialization? The singer-actors train to perform a particular type of repertory closely related to opera and operetta. Yes, theatrical singers use microphones to amplify their voices; they have to sing eight shows a week. If opera stars sang that often without amplification, their voices would be in tatters. Most limit themselves to three performances a week to give their voices a chance to recover. When opera is performed outdoors, all singers mic up. Does that mean that they are now singing a musical? Some opera houses also occasionally use amplification, though they don't publicize the fact. Practical issues are not aesthetic principles.

Finally, there is the objection that *Sweeney Todd* comes out of popular musical theater and not the classical tradition. Isn't this the silliest and most parochial objection of all? The classical tradition is omnivorous. For centuries it has refreshed itself by borrowing from popular culture as well as internal refinements. Chopin transformed Polish dance rhythms, the mazurka and polonaise, into classical forms. Vaughan Williams and Holst, Bartók and Kodály made symphonic and vocal works from folk tunes and modal scales. Domenico Scarlatti added Spanish folk guitar flourishes to his classical keyboard sonatas. Gershwin, Stravinsky, and Milhaud used jazz rhythms and harmonies. Philip Glass employed rock bass beats. The list is as long as the history of classical music. Some denounce such borrowing as cultural appropriation; most see it as the creative conversation between cultures and classes. There is nothing new or wrong in such transformative borrowing; it drives innovation. Nearly all American music has been shaped by such fusion, none more so than classical composers who follow European models.

This objection to Sondheim is a sort of professional snobbery. What annoys some detractors is that it wasn't a classical composer who did the borrowing. The new synthesis came from an artist working in the popular form who developed ways to order and intensify his medium until it had the force and integrity of classical opera. To relegate Sondheim to an inferior category of composer isn't merely ill-advised, it's fatuous. He had musical training, a lifetime of professional experience, international recognition, and genius. Even in the Music Department, genius should count for something.

The counter-argument that *Sweeney Todd* is an opera can be summarized simply. The work is now widely presented in opera houses performed by operatic casts and symphonic orchestras. Its reception has not merely been favorable; it's been rapturous. Its success reveals how hungry the operatic audience has been for powerful and engrossing new works. The show works in opera houses not only because of the compelling quality of the score and lyrics. *Sweeney Todd* is a tragedy, a genre more familiar to the opera house than to musical theater. As Terry Teachout observed at the Royal Opera House opening in London, "Sweeney is a genuinely tragic figure, a man driven mad by his longing for revenge not merely on those individuals who have wronged him but on an entire society that he takes to be poisoned by hypocrisy." No one who has seen *Rigoletto* will find that premise unfamiliar.

If *Sweeney Todd* succeeds in both the theater and the opera house, it is also unnerving in both venues. The work is too dark for musical theater, too grossly funny for opera. It has a vulgarity and violence unusual for both. Todd's first song begins:

> There is a hole in the world
> Like a great black pit

And the vermin of the world
Inhabit it,
And its morals aren't worth
What a pig could spit
And it goes by the name of London.

Sweeney Todd wouldn't work in either venue if the humor and horror weren't so perfectly integrated to create a credible tragic style. *Sweeney Todd* is a literary triumph: American opera has no better libretto. Sondheim's verse is wickedly sharp and sometimes startling. Its humor makes the horror bearable and the malefactors human. Its horror makes the violence feel more real than it normally does on an operatic stage. Being buried alive seems beautiful in *Aida*. Death is never pretty in *Sweeney Todd*. The show makes its strongest impression sung by classically trained voices with a large symphony, if the singers have clear diction. The weight of the voices and orchestra makes the tragic horror more tangible and immediate.

Sweeney Todd isn't just an opera. With *Porgy and Bess*, it is one of the two best operas in American music. It is not coincidental that both works draw power from popular music. They are stronger and fresher for their mixed ancestry. It is naïve to believe American opera will become more vital by clinging to elite inbreeding. *Porgy* and *Sweeney Todd* remind us how many of the most enduring American operas began on Broadway or television. The two works also demonstrate the importance of strong and memorable lyrics for English-language opera. How much we lose when the words are indifferently written or indistinctly set. Poetry enlarges the meaning of dramatic music more precisely and memorably than instrumental scene-setting. The splendor of opera is the fusion of music, poetry, and drama made manifest by the human voice. Opera will never be so sophisticated that it does not need song.

CHAPTER XXIII

A Tale of Two Librettists

Literature, in the form of the text to be
set to music, must always be ready to
help the composer; whether music can
help literature is another matter.

—ANTHONY BURGESS

OPERA IS THE ONLY LIVING FORM OF POETIC DRAMA—the last corner of theater in which the poet remains a necessary collaborator. Although opera has declined in influence and visibility over the past century, it continues to develop as an art form—still supported by a sizable and devoted audience. The operatic repertory consists mostly of classic works, but hundreds of contemporary operas are produced each year. Many of these works are world premieres—produced not only in opera houses but also in universities, conservatories, festivals, and performance spaces. Most of the new operas are still written, entirely or partially, in verse.

Opera is also the only surviving form of tragic theater. It remains a dramatic medium driven by the direct presentation and virtuosic articulation of powerful emotions. No one suffers silently in opera. It has never lost its fascination for expressing the extremes of human suffering. If a contemporary poet wants to create a verse tragedy, there are only two practical options—translate a classic or write for the opera house.

The uncomfortable question is whether all this new operatic creation has much to do with literature. How many new libretti have any poetic merit? Is the libretto still a genre of aesthetic significance or does it survive only as a historical relic? Few opera impresarios or directors make claims for the literary merit of the texts they commission. They might even be puzzled by the question. "Literary quality is irrelevant," declared critic Terry Teachout. Isn't a libretto merely the blueprint for a production that requires sets, costumes, and direction to communicate its full meaning? Don't all these elements matter less than the music? A poet who wishes to write a libretto of genuine merit must accept that the music world does not share that goal.

Literary quality is no guarantee of operatic success. Consider the careers of two contemporary poets turned librettists. No living librettist is more talented than James Fenton. The poet had extraordinary success in musical theater early in his career. He helped craft English lyrics for Alain Boublil and Claude-Michel Schönberg's mega-hit *Les Misérables*. Although Fenton was dropped from the creative team, enough of his "additional material" was used to earn him several million pounds in royalties. Meanwhile he had translated performing versions of *Rigoletto* and *Simon Boccanegra* for English National Opera. No poet seemed better poised for future operatic success.

Fenton then wrote *The Love Bomb*, an original libretto for composer Thomas Adès for what appeared to be a major commission. Adès had enjoyed broad success with his first opera, *Powder Her Face* (1995), and the British musical press had anointed him the successor to Benjamin Britten. Adès felt uncomfortable about the subject of Fenton's libretto, a Christian cult. He asked for significant revisions, disliked the results which included a homosexual subplot. Adès then canceled the project. He approached Fenton about an alternative idea, a new version of Shakespeare's *The Tempest*. When Fenton submitted sample sections, Adès rejected them for being too literary. The composer soon commissioned a simplified version of the play from Meredith Oakes—a version of Shakespeare's play without Shakespeare's language.

After his two failures with Adès, Fenton wrote *Haroun and the Sea of Stories* (based on a short novel by Salman Rushdie) for composer Charles Wuorinen. The New York City Opera premiered the work in 2004. Wuorinen, the aging prince of the academic avantgarde, produced a severe and tuneless score unlikely to earn a place in posterity. Even Wuorinen's considerable influence couldn't secure a second staged production. Fenton has written no more libretti.

David Mason's operatic career began modestly. He collaborated with composer Lori Laitman on her first full-length opera, *The Scarlet Letter* (2008), which was premiered at the University of Central Arkansas. The venue had little prestige, but the school staged a strong production. The powerfully dramatic work was so well received that Opera Colorado performed and recorded a revised version which has gone on to three more productions.

Meanwhile Mason wrote two original one-act libretti, *After Life* (2015) and *The Parting* (2019) for Tom Cipullo. These unusual dramas resemble Japanese Noh plays, though Mason probably did not conceive of them in such terms: they are conversations with ghosts. *After Life* has three characters, all posthumous—Gertrude Stein, Pablo Picasso, and an unnamed girl killed in the Holocaust. *The Parting* depicts the last night the Hungarian poet Miklós Radnóti spent with his wife before his conscription for forced labor by the Nazis. Radnóti is still alive in the opera, but he knows his death is imminent and only his poems will survive him. Both operas have had multiple productions and recordings. Mason and Laitman are currently working on *Ludlow*, an opera about the 1914 massacre of striking coal miners in Colorado.

A librettist is at the mercy of the composer. Fenton was lucky in his royalties, but Mason fortunate in his partners.

CHAPTER XXIV

Putting It Together

*Opera is the last refuge
of the High Style.*

—W. H. AUDEN

CHRISTOPH WILLIBALD GLUCK'S VISION OF OPERA AS-
sumed a collaboration so complete that neither the
words nor the music could be judged separately from
the other. "The union between the words and the singing [must] be so close that the poem should not appear
to be less composed for the music, than the music for
the poem." Gluck's theory is persuasive in the abstract,
but its exalted view of an ideal finished work offers little
practical guidance to a poet beginning a libretto.

Creating words for opera, a poet faces different
demands than in writing for the page. "The first duty of
the librettist," wrote Auden and Kallman, "is, needless
to say, to write verses which excite the musical imagination of the composer; if these verses should also possess
poetic merit in themselves, so much the better, but such
merit is a secondary consideration." This formulation
neatly captures the poet's dilemma. The crucial audi-

ence for a libretto is neither the reader nor operagoer but the composer. The poetic text exists to be transformed into music. Sometimes that transformation is violent. While composing *Aida*, Verdi sent his librettist Antonio Ghislanzoni a radically cut and changed version of one scene. "I know what you will say," wrote the composer, "'and what has become of verse, rhyme, and stanza?' I don't know what to answer you. I only know that whenever the action demanded it, I would at once abandon rhythm, rhyme, and stanza."

Crafting a libretto, a poet recognizes various practical issues. The language must be less dense than verse written for the page. The lyrics need to be emotionally direct and easily sung. Intelligibility is a constant challenge; even good singers can't convey every word of the text. (As Strauss warned, "A third of the words nearly always get lost.") The poet must also do something unthinkable in literary terms: write lines that register their basic meaning even when some of the words get garbled. Intricate wordplay will be lost in the singing.

Not all of those requirements are disagreeable. In opera, the poet enjoys the luxury of writing more simply because the words need not communicate everything. The text is only part of a libretto; there are also stage directions and settings. Important things can be communicated by movement, pantomime, and staging. Stagecraft is alien to poets; they have spent years learning how to write words that need no scenic assistance.

Finally, the finished lines need to be porous, sometimes even incomplete, to leave room for the composer.

If the lyrics are too rich or densely textured—which are usually good things on the page—they may resist musical setting. Eventually music will dominate every element in the libretto. It will support, deepen, and often transform the meaning of the words. It will also add much of the nuance the poet normally puts on the page. While the poet creates—or at least initiates—the story, characters, situations, and sentiments of the drama, it is the composer who brings them alive on stage.

A libretto can be too richly written. It can't be coincidental that nearly all of the enduring operas based on Shakespeare have been done in foreign languages. Verdi's *Otello*, *Macbeth*, and *Falstaff*, Charles Gounod's *Roméo et Juliette*, Ambroise Thomas's *Hamlet*, and Otto Nicolai's *Die Lustigen Weiber von Windsor* have survived in the repertory while no English language adaptation has yet demonstrated its longevity—not even those by Vaughan Williams, Britten, or Barber. Shakespeare's verse has too much distinctive music of its own in the original to be comfortably set. When Thomas Adès set *The Tempest*, he had the text rewritten in shorter lines and simpler language—which is to say, he had the poetry removed.

The poet's challenge is to provide the composer with enough depth but not too much detail. What is enough and not too little? The composer probably understands the right verbal texture better than the poet. Those big, bold lines that seem shamefully naked to a poet are often those that the composer instinctively knows how to clothe most magnificently in music. Paradoxically, the less important lines need to be boldly written since no powerful musical idea will support them.

Once the text has been transformed into a musical score, a second radical transformation occurs: the work is performed by other artists. Without singers, the score remains a stack of silent pages. In performance the work changes its mode of existence—and not simply from mute notation into sound. The work moves from spatial to temporal existence; it unfolds as a complex series of expressive actions for a finite amount of time. "Art is not thought or emotion," Willa Cather wrote, "but expression, expression, always expression." Opera does not fully exist except in performance. Moreover, the singers not only perform the work; they interpret it and thereby change or at least color the meaning. No two singers convey exactly the same meaning.

I said earlier that the poet writes words for the composer, but that is only partially true. The poet also writes for the singers. The lines of a libretto fully exist only when they are sung. While writing the lyrics, the poet must summon up characters who will speak those lines. The composer then makes it credible—indeed inevitable—that the characters would sing the lines. Playwrights always write words for other people to speak. That is their special craft. To poets, the situation is unnerving. They have spent years finding their own voice, not creating dialogue for others. In public, poets recite their own words to present their own personality and vision. Writing compact and memorable lyrics that allow singers to express their fictive selves is a challenge.

Operatic verse differs from literary poetry because it exists in a different medium. It is sung not spoken; it is performed not read. It offers the same meanings and pleasures as poetry but in a form malleable enough for the composer to set it to music. A libretto can and will be read on the page, but it can only be judged in its final form as theatrical music in performance when the words are vocalized and interpreted by a cast of singers.

How neatly stacked the odds are against the poet writing a distinguished libretto. The text must satisfy the conflicting demands of the composer, singers, and audience. It must present a clear and compelling narrative while also constantly providing emotional situations for lyrical expression. The words must be poetic but not so rich as to block the composer's own inspiration. The language needs to be mostly intelligible when sung. The verse must be concise but nonetheless unfold a drama of psychological depth. And, finally, no one except the poet cares if the words are more than serviceable.

CHAPTER XXV

Personal Drama

NINA: *Your play's hard to act,*
there are no living people in it.

TREPLEV: *Living people!*
We should show life neither
as it is nor as it ought to be,
but as we see it in our dreams.

—ANTON CHEKHOV, *THE SEAGULL*

WHY DID I WRITE MY FIRST OPERA LIBRETTO? IT WASN'T for lack of anything else to do. I was already overcommitted when composer Alva Henderson approached me. Neither was the attraction financial; Henderson did not have a commission. Literary reputation played no part in the decision. My fellow poets had little interest in contemporary classical music, and the libretto commanded no prestige in the literary world.

Yet my interest was immediate. Once the composer had mentioned the impractical and unremunerative project, an opera libretto seemed exactly what I wanted—and indeed *needed*—to do. The idea felt all the more appealing because the form was so *outré*. I was also a little stage-struck. I had just finished two theatrical ventures—a full-length dance theater piece with the Mark Ruhala Performance Group based on my poem "Counting the Children," and a Verse Theater Manhattan production of my translation of Seneca's *The Madness of Hercules*. Seeing those pieces performed, I had been excited by the possibilities of poetic theater. How many interesting things one might do by mixing poetry, music, and drama.

What intrigued me most about opera was the chance to explore poetic drama. Could a writer still create a compelling theater work with credible characters in the heightened language of poetry? It was a perilous project to attempt in spoken theater. Shakespearean ambition had been the downfall of numerous modern poets. The verse dramas of Delmore Schwartz, Archibald MacLeish, Edna St. Vincent Millay, and E. E. Cummings make painful reading. Ever since the Romantic era, when poetry began to focus on interior psychology, verse drama has had little theatrical success. The poetic tragedies of Keats, Byron, and Shelley—not to mention those of Longfellow, Tennyson, Arnold, and Swinburne—were a procession of artistic and theatrical failures. I have never seen any of these famous flops produced, but I've enjoyed their best scenes and passages. What poet can read *Prometheus Unbound*, *The Cenci*, or *Manfred* without staging these eloquent but awkward plays in the theater of one's imagination? None of them, however, cry out for revival.

I've been more impressed by the intermittent modern tradition, which had some estimable successes in the verse dramas of Yeats, Eliot, Jeffers, and Auden. Robinson Jeffers's *Medea* is an unqualified masterpiece, the best modern verse play in American literature, but it has the authority of Euripides behind it. *Purgatory*, *Murder in the Cathedral*, and *The Ascent of F6* are imperfect plays but each has touches of genius. I admire Christopher Fry's verse comedies, especially *The Lady's Not for Burning* and *Venus Observed*, but his language is too silver-tongued and smooth to go deeply into the human heart. (More recently, there have been fine verse plays by Derek Walcott, Tony Harrison, and David Ives.) These plays display aspects of each author's imagination not evident in their other work. New forms open new avenues for expression.

I had wondered, however, if words alone could still suffice for poetic drama. Back in high school, I had an LP of Yeats's *The Only Jealousy of Emer* with a musical score by Lou Harrison. The simple but bewitching musical accompaniment intensified the dream-like drama. How sly Yeats had been to insist his *Plays for Dancers* include the ritual elements of music, mime, and movement. "I have invented a form of drama, distinguished, indirect, and symbolic," he rightly boasted. W. H. Auden and Christopher Isherwood asked the young Benjamin Britten to write songs and incidental music for their verse plays, *Ascent of F6* and *On the Frontier*. The Group Theatre's director, Rupert Doone, a trained dancer, added choreography. The music and dance gave resonance to the verbally brilliant but dramatically thin plays. Few readers realize that some of Auden's most popular poems began as theatrical songs:

> Stop all the clocks, cut off the telephone,
> Prevent the dog from barking with a juicy bone,
> Silence the pianos and with muffled drum
> Bring out the coffin, let the mourners come.

I saw the powerful interplay between poetry and dance when Mark Ruhala staged *Counting the Children*. I had been skeptical that my long and complex poem could work as a dance piece, but the choreography, music, and staging made it immediate and accessible. Spoken in its entirety by the lead dancer, the text became transparent to the audience—who were not people who generally read poetry. The music and movement created a non-verbal text parallel to my words. For me, the primary appeal of opera and dance lay in their ritual elements. Music allows the audience to experience the words not intellectually but physically, emotionally, and intuitively. The poet can try things beyond what might work on the page.

Another impulse that led me to opera was the excitement of collaboration, which is so different from the solitary labor of writing. Working with other artists is not easy. The pleasure is mixed with anxiety, frustration, and disagreement, but shared labor nurtures deep friendship. In my case, collaboration also heightens my sense of urgency. I am a slow writer: I often take a single poem through dozens of drafts over several years before I show it to anyone. I sometimes choose not to publish it at all.

Writing a libretto required me to finish every song and scene—although not always on time and rarely in the order they would appear on the stage. I was also aware that every syllable I wrote would be studied and weighed by the composer. Then every line in the final score would be sung by another human being who would have to portray the character suggested by the words. I found these unusual demands invigorating. I resolved to write poetry that would be equally interesting on the page and on the stage—though perhaps in different ways. Here, for example, is the opening of the vampire's aria of seduction from *Nosferatu*:

I am the image that darkens your glass,
The shadow that falls wherever you pass.
I am the dream you cannot forget,
The face you remember without having met.

I am the truth that must not be spoken,
The midnight vow that cannot be broken.
I am the bell that tolls out the hours.
I am the fire that warms and devours.

I wouldn't have agreed to write a libretto had I not loved Henderson's music. Real collaboration requires mutual esteem. For opera, it's even more than that; it requires a sort of creative romance. There are librettists who can happily supply a text on demand. I'm not one of them. I need to be fascinated, in advance, by the music my collaborator can call into existence. A libretto is a love letter to the composer's imagination. It woos him or her into confabulation. It brings the characters and their words into a fantasy world the poet and composer share. Their *folie à deux* must grow large enough to accommodate a cast, a crew, and eventually the public.

When I first heard Henderson's one-act opera, *The Last Leaf,* at New York University in 1979, I recognized him as a rare talent who wrote with brilliant expressivity for the voice. He also had a natural sense of theater. His characters felt alive. And he composed moving and memorable melodies. After hearing his *Medea* (1972), which uses Jeffers's powerful version of Euripides' tragedy, and *The Last of the Mohicans* (1976) with its libretto by Janet Lewis, I was convinced. We were close enough in style and vision to make collaboration possible but sufficiently different in temperament to make partnership interesting.

My subsequent operatic projects with Paul Salerni and Lori Laitman also began with admiration for their music. I did not at first know either composer personally. Both had asked me for permission to set a poem of mine to music. I liked the songs so much that we did other projects. The idea of writing an opera emerged slowly; it was a serious decision. Operas take years to plan, write, and premiere. One needs the right partners. It's not just a project; it's a marriage.

In each case, I made an unusual demand. I asked to

choose the subject of the opera. The composer could veto my suggestions, but I needed a story and an imaginative world that I could inhabit for the years it took to complete the project. In the music world, my request is considered outrageous—a librettist exists to do the impresario and composer's bidding. I am frequently struck by the flavorless quality of many new commissions. It is obvious that the composer or general director dictated a subject for which the librettist had no deep affinity. The resulting texts are professionally executed but imaginatively stillborn. If you believe that a good text inspires better music—and I do—then there needs to be some genuine poetic spark to ignite the project.

I have written my libretti in an odd way that—to my surprise—usually mirrored the composer's process. I drafted many of the scenes out of order. The total action of the opera had already been plotted, scene by scene, in a prose summary. I would write the opening scene to establish the style and approach—and to let the composer give me his or her suggestions. Then I would craft the later scenes by writing the peak moments first, often a central aria or duet. I wanted to give the emotional highpoint of the scene independent poetic energy. Lyric drama must have lyric power. Only after finishing the high point, would I write everything that led up to and away from that moment. The composers liked to work this way, too—composing the major themes first and then developing them across the scene.

I happened upon the subject of *Nosferatu* by accident. I had lunch one day with the film critic Gilberto

Perez. He showed me an essay he had just written on F. W. Murnau's film. I learned from Perez that I had never seen the director's original version, only a severely cut print made for export. Perez gave me his essay, "The Deadly Space Between," and loaned me a videotape of the full *Nosferatu*. Watching the complete film, I was struck by how much Murnau's Expressionist tale of horror resembled a bel canto tragic opera. Surely the director had thought of his film in musical terms; he subtitled *Nosferatu* "A Symphony in Grays," and wrote the screenplay-scenario in verse.

Although Murnau borrowed his basic plot from Bram Stoker's *Dracula* (which he could not legally obtain the rights to film), he simplified the story in ways that made it dramatically stronger and more resonantly symbolic. *Nosferatu* offered a librettist the positive virtues of a compelling plot, strong characters, and vivid—indeed, often unforgettable—images. The silent film also afforded the important negative virtues of having neither spoken words nor music. How astonishing that the Dracula legend, one of the great Romantic myths, had never served as the subject of an enduring opera. (Heinrich Marschner's rarely performed 1828 opera, *Der Vampyr*, is not about vampirism in the modern sense of the word.) Murnau's *Nosferatu* provided a resonant but compressed version of the Dracula myth in a dramatization that left room for poetry and music.

As a child, I loved horror movies, which I knew mostly from television. On weekends, my cousins and

I would gather to watch the local station broadcast the black and white Universal films of the early talkie era— *Dracula* (1931), *Frankenstein* (1931), *The Wolfman* (1941), *The Mummy* (1932), and our collective favorite, *The Bride of Frankenstein* (1935). The old films must have been inexpensive to license because they were constantly replayed. In those pre-digital days, we watched every airing—often mouthing the dialogue along with Bela Lugosi or Boris Karloff. Meanwhile, I read the various movie histories in the local library and bought—to my parents' horror—each new issue of *Famous Monsters of Filmland*.

These sources led me to German silent horror and fantasy films such as Fritz Lang's *Metropolis* (1926), Robert Wiene's *The Cabinet of Dr. Caligari* (1920), and Murnau's *Nosferatu* (1922), all of which I managed to see by age twelve. (Los Angeles offered advantages to juvenile film buffs in those pre-internet days, including a silent movie TV program and the nation's last commercial silent film theater.) *Nosferatu* became a part of my working-class, Latin-Catholic childhood. I first watched it as a horror movie and not a classic of German Expressionist cinema.

Perhaps for that reason, working on the libretto touched other childhood memories of religion, family, and poverty. I recalled my beautiful Aunt Felice dying of cancer, the *Salve Regina* being recited at the end of my parochial school's daily morning mass, and my family's constant worries about money. These childhood events intermingled naturally with my first sighting of

Max Schreck's shadow climbing the stairway toward his shuddering victim. I had never written about these early experiences. This was the creative gift of writing a libretto—the new form invited new subjects and different styles. *Nosferatu* is full of poetry I would not have written under other circumstances. The dramatic form had another advantage. I could disguise my life as part of someone else's story since the underlying myth was big enough to hold us all.

To write a libretto that might also succeed as poetic drama is to bet against the odds. Worse yet, it takes long odds for low stakes. But isn't that the precondition of all poetry today? Writing poetry risks overwhelming odds of failure. And if one succeeds, how few people notice. There is nothing new about this bleak insight. Even Milton questioned the wisdom of dedicating one's life to "the thankless Muse." Verse is a vocation without notable rewards. "Poetry is not a career," said T. S. Eliot, "but a mug's game."

Why complain? Isn't the impractical and unprofitable nature of poetry part of its splendor? In a world where everything has a price, poetry still exists outside the marketplace. A beautiful, endangered beast, it survives, like a snow leopard or panda, beyond the margins of the practical world of profits and prose.

Why bother to write at all, except for the joy of work and fresh discovery? Robert Frost called poetry the highest kind of enterprise, "a self-appointed task," where "hard labor comes from one's own desire and internal pressure for perfection." Writing a libretto adds to poetry the pleasure of collaboration. It is a hard game, two to a side, played against indifference and oblivion. We may lose in the long run, but until then, it is the finest sport a poet and composer can find.

ACKNOWLEDGMENTS

This book grew slowly in fits and starts over many years. Parts of it originated in commentary I provided as an afterword to my libretto for *Nosferatu*. The ideas in that piece struck me as interesting but undeveloped. Ten years later, at the University of Southern California's Thornton School of Music, I created a graduate course for singers and composers on "Words and Music." We studied the texts and scores of opera, lieder, and cabaret; the singers also performed classics as well as new vocal works by the class composers. I eventually wrote a long essay exploring the subject, but it seemed too long to include in a critical collection. I thank the editorial staff at Paul Dry Books for the initial suggestion that I should expand the piece into its own book, as well as for their subsequent work on the project.

I also want to thank three poets—in Orvieto, Tulsa, and Tasmania—who came to my aid. Andrew Frisardi read an early version of the book and offered excellent advice. Boris Dralyuk and David Mason read individual chapters which they improved with their comments. I am grateful to Philip Le Masurier for allowing us to reprint his unforgettable photograph on the cover of this book. (And I thank the indefatigable Douglas Hassall for locating Le Masurier in Sydney, Australia.) My wife, Mary, who hates to be thanked, helped me at every stage of composition. Finally, I thank Paula Deitz, who published two sections in the *Hudson Review*. Her support—and that of her late husband and co-editor Frederick Morgan—deserves a double aria of appreciation. Years ago, I dedicated a book to both of them. This volume is for Paula.

INDEX OF NAMES AND TITLES

ABOUT THE AUTHOR

Dana Gioia is the former Poet Laureate of California. He has published six collections of verse, including *Interrogations at Noon* (2001), which won the American Book Award, and *99 Poems: New & Selected* (2016), which won the Poets' Prize. His critical collections include *Can Poetry Matter?* (1992), which was a finalist for the National Book Critics Award. His most recent book is *Meet Me at the Lighthouse* (2023).

Gioia has worked with many classical and jazz composers, including Morten Lauridsen, James MacMillan, Lori Laitman, Ned Rorem, Alva Henderson, Paul Salerni, Stefania de Kenessey, Tom Cipullo, David Felder, Paquito D'Rivera, and Dave Brubeck. He collaborated with jazz pianist Helen Sung on her first vocal album, *Sung with Words*.

He has written five opera libretti, including *Nosferatu* (2004) with Alva Henderson; *Tony Caruso's Final Broadcast* (2010) and *Haunted* (2019), a dance opera, with Paul Salerni; and *The Three Feathers* (2014) and *Maya and the Magic Ring* (2025) with Lori Laitman.

Gioia served as Chairman of the National Endowment for the Arts where he launched the largest programs in the agency's history. He has been praised as "the man who saved the NEA." He has received Notre Dame's Laetare Medal, the Aiken-Taylor Award in Modern Poetry, and the Presidential Citizen's Medal. For nine years, Gioia was the Judge Widney Professor of Poetry and Public Culture at the University of Southern California.

He divides his time between Los Angeles and Sonoma County, California.